D0959920

Officially Withdrawn

John F. Reed Library
Fort Lewis College
Durango, Colorado 81301

PENGUIN CLASSICS

THE HISTORY OF RASSELAS,
PRINCE OF ABISSINIA

SAMUEL JOHNSON was born in Lichfield in 1709, the son of a book-seller, and was educated at Lichfield Grammar School and, for a short time, at Pembroke College, Oxford. He taught for a while, after which he worked for a Birmingham printer, for whom he translated Lobo's *A Voyage to Abyssinia*. In 1735 he married Elizabeth Jervis Porter and with her money opened a boarding academy. The school was a failure and in 1737 Johnson left for London. There, he became a regular contributor to the *Gentleman's Magazine* and struggled to earn a living from writing. But it was not until the award of a government pension in 1762 that Johnson gained financial security. His *London: A Poem in Imitation of the Third Satire of Juvenal* was published anonymously in 1738 and attracted some attention. *The Vanity of Human Wishes: The Tenth Satire of Juvenal Imitated* appeared under his own name in 1749. From 1750 to 1752 he issued the *Rambler*, a periodical written almost entirely by himself, and consolidated his position as a notable moral essayist with some twenty-five essays in the *Adventurer*. The *Idler* essays, lighter in tone, appeared weekly between 1758 and 1760. When his *Dictionary of the English Language* was published in 1755, Johnson took on the proportions of a literary monarch in the London of his day. In need of money to visit his sick mother, he wrote *Rasselas* (1759) reportedly in the evenings of one week, finishing a couple of days after his mother's death. In 1763 Boswell became his faithful follower and it is mainly to his *Life* that we owe our intimate knowledge of Johnson. Founded in 1764, 'The Club' (of literary men) was the perfect forum for the exercise of Johnson's great conversational art. His edition of Shakespeare's plays appeared in 1765. From August to November 1773 he and Boswell toured Scotland and in 1775 his *Journey to the Western Islands of Scotland* appeared. His last major work was *Lives of the Poets*. He died in December 1784.

D. J. ENRIGHT has taught at a number of universities and sub-sequently worked in publishing. His publications include *English Critical Texts*, *Shakespeare and the Students*, *Fields of Vision* and *Collected Poems 1987*, and he edited *The Oxford Book of Death*.

SAMUEL JOHNSON

The History of Rasselas, Prince of Abissinia

Edited with an introduction by
D. J. Enright

PENGUIN BOOKS

PENGUIN BOOKS

Published by the Penguin Group
Penguin Books Ltd, 27 Wrights Lane, London W8 5TZ, England
Penguin Books USA Inc., 375 Hudson Street, New York, New York 10014, USA
Penguin Books Australia Ltd, Ringwood, Victoria, Australia
Penguin Books Canada Ltd, 10 Alcorn Avenue, Toronto, Ontario, Canada M4V 3B2
Penguin Books (NZ) Ltd, 182–190 Wairau Road, Auckland 10, New Zealand

Penguin Books Ltd, Registered Offices: Harmondsworth, Middlesex, England

First published in 1959
Published in Penguin Books 1976
Reprinted in Penguin Classics 1985
9 10 8

Introduction and notes copyright © D. J. Enright, 1976
All rights reserved

Printed in England by Clays Ltd, St Ives plc
Set in Monotype Garamond

Except in the United States of America, this book is sold subject
to the condition that it shall not, by way of trade or otherwise, be lent,
re-sold, hired out, or otherwise circulated without the publisher's
prior consent in any form of binding or cover other than that in
which it is published and without a similar condition including this
condition being imposed on the subsequent purchaser

CONTENTS

Contents

Contents

INTRODUCTION

I

'WE are perpetually moralists, but we are geometricians only by chance,' Samuel Johnson remarked in his *Life of Milton*. Undoubtedly *Rasselas* is a moral tale, whether or not Johnson was a novelist only by chance. His comment on the novelist Richardson – that if we were to read him for the story, our impatience would be so much fretted that we should hang ourselves – is one we may be tempted to apply to *Rasselas*. I say 'may be tempted', since it is unlikely that a string of apophthegms *in vacuo*, a row of pegs on which to hang wise counsels, could have anything like the enormous and widespread appeal that *Rasselas* has exerted over the years. There must be a story inside it: a simple, primitive, basic one, like the story inside that highly sophisticated work of Thomas Mann's, *The Magic Mountain*; and characters too, though stripped of all 'accidentals', which emerge distinguishably and (though without losing their 'representative' quality) even develop in the course of the story. But if not exactly for the story, as we had better admit, we read *Rasselas* for the solidity of its wisdom (a more tolerant kind, it should be said, than is sometimes supposed) and the verbal force and skill with which that wisdom is pressed home, out of our realization that the author is concerned with fundamentals rather than incidentals (there are still readers who consider this a compliment), and for its humour.

Remembering the expectation of a load of gloom which, as Paul Fussell has commented, the traditional association of *Rasselas* with the death of Johnson's mother has encouraged some readers to form, we might have done better to start with these humorous stanzas of Johnson's:

> Hermit hoar, in solemn cell,
>   Wearing out life's evening grey:
> Smite thy bosom, sage, and tell,
>   What is bliss? and which the way?

> Thus I spoke; and speaking sigh'd;
> – Scarce repress'd the starting tear; –
> When the smiling sage reply'd –
> – Come, my lad, and drink some beer.

In fact, this is a parody of Thomas Warton and, more generally, indicates Johnson's contemptuous view of the 'Gothic', the romantic or pre-romantic afflatus in all its forms. But its solemn question, 'What is bliss? and which the way?', could stand as quizzical epigraph to *Rasselas*, for while Johnson's answer is not quite as hearty as the smiling sage's, our author is not intending to smite his bosom. One 'romantic' phenomenon of his time was the oriental tale, the *Arabian Nights Entertainments* and the *Persian Tales*, with its fairy-tale exoticism and allegoricism, an escape from the 'age of reason', from Grub Street and from the British weather. Johnson's treatment of the oriental genre is in the mode governing his lines about the 'hermit hoar'. He was, as part of his strategy, de-romanticizing: primarily, of course, de-romanticizing highflown and ignorantly optimistic ideas about life, and only secondarily deflating the expectations set up by a tale about the mysterious East. 'If Coleridge's magic damsel with a dulcimer were some-how to make an appearance in *Rasselas*, we should laugh,' says Mr Fussell. Yes, but very likely we should hear some-thing accurate and informative about the manipulation and function of the dulcimer and the working conditions of the damsel.

But Johnson had already made the point about Eastern fantasies. In 1735, twenty-four years earlier, he had pub-lished an abridged translation of the Jesuit Father Jeronymo Lobo's *Voyage to Abyssinia*, and in the preface to this he noted that

> ... the Portuguese traveller ... has amused his reader with no romantic absurdities or incredible fictions: whatever he relates, whether true or not, is at least probable ... He appears ... to have copied nature from the life, and to have consulted his senses, not his imagination. He meets with no basilisks that destroy with their eyes; his crocodiles devour their prey without

tears; and his cataracts fall from the rock without deafening the neighbouring inhabitants.

The reader will here find no regions cursed with irremediable barrenness, or blest with spontaneous fecundity; no perpetual gloom, or unceasing sunshine; nor are the nations here described either devoid of all sense of humanity, or consummate in all private and social virtues: here are no Hottentots without religion, polity, or articulate language; no Chinese perfectly polite and completely skilled in all sciences . . .

Johnson concluded this vindication of his interest in Lobo's book by remarking that the reader will discover in it 'what will always be discovered by a diligent and impartial inquirer, that wherever human nature is to be found, there is a mixture of vice and virtue, a contest of passion and reason . . .' This is what the reader of *Rasselas*, like the travellers in that book, is to discover, together with the discrepancy between what is wished for and what is obtained.

Johnson's thought is drawn by the horses of instruction rather than the tigers of wrath, to use Blake's distinction: on his intellectual map the road of excess led to the gutter or the lunatic asylum. That was because he knew about wrath and madness, not because he was cosily ignorant or obtusely reactionary. Knowledge and information and fact he always prized; fantasy and imagination he feared, with the fear of a man who knows the horrors and disasters they can unleash: his agonized response to the death of Cordelia, the murder of Desdemona and the suicide of Ophelia, makes Shakespearean commentators ostensibly more 'feeling' look deficient in imaginative participation or even thick-skinned. It is one's awareness of intense pressures, evinced as they must be in his peculiar blend of large abstractions and poignant specificities, which marks Johnson out as something quite other than a simple-minded champion of rationalism or a mouthpiece for formalized moderation. The tigers are there all right, and the reader had better be informed that they have teeth and claws. Johnson was a 'poetic', a metaphorical, writer –

that's to say, he had imagination and he used it – but he believed that untruths and fancies weakened, and that only the truth, though it might not make us free, could make us strong. In *Rasselas* the result is a work which, as John Wain says, 'puts one in mind of a dragonfly – a purposeful and powerful body moving on wings of gauze'.

I hope it will not sound lowering to describe *Rasselas* as a conducted tour of truths and untruths, so long as we add that it is an exploratory and not altogether predetermined tour. Seeking to correct the view of the book as the expression and 'happy illustration' of set and settled doctrine, John Wiltshire has put it this way: '*Rasselas* will seem less inspired by a desire to teach or modify manners and morals on grounds which Johnson is sure of, than a pondering of doubts and questions.' It is, I would suggest, a homogeneous or 'natural'-seeming blend, in which the ingredients are not always immediately recognizable, of firm certainties with persistent doubts and pondered questions. It would be vain to seek to defend the work against the charge of being 'episodic': it is not a charge which is pertinent here. Nor will it do to complain of, or seek to excuse, the shortness of the book's chapters. The chapters are so weighty, their specific gravity is so high, that the reader is positively appreciative of their brevity. It is not that he fails to read on, but he does experience a relief analogous to that of putting down one solid object before picking up the next. And the next is commonly a new one. That is, the chapter-breaks stress the sense of variety and also the sense of active engagement in the work, which would be weaker without them. Like the blank spaces between aphorisms, they allow one to think over what has been said before continuing. A good brandy should not be taken in tumblers.

2

The episodic and aphoristic procedure makes it difficult to talk usefully about *Rasselas* in any way other than that of the progressive or running commentary. We shall have to begin at the beginning.

'Ye who listen with credulity to the whispers of fancy, and pursue with eagerness the phantoms of hope . . .' The beginning has been much admired, and indeed the mixture of plangency in the opening of that first sentence and of stern briskness in the close ('attend to the history of Rasselas prince of Abissinia') provides an attractive index to the overall tone of the book. One may have doubts about Mr Fussell's claim that the opening establishes *Rasselas* as 'virtually a boy's book', despite his adduction of Johnson's anxiety in *Rambler* 4 about the effects of fiction on 'the young, the ignorant, and the idle . . . minds unfurnished with ideas, and therefore easily susceptible of impressions'. True, the prince himself and his friends are young, or fairly young: the recipient of wise counsels is traditionally represented as young and with, ostensibly, all before him, and the giver of them as old and with much behind him, but (I would surmise) one does not get the impression that Johnson is really addressing himself to any special age-group. Men can deceive themselves or be deceived at any age – furnished or unfurnished with ideas, experienced or otherwise, no age is immune to the human condition. *Rasselas* contains too much pathos and too much resignation to be an unambiguously effective clarion call to successful living. It is no more 'a boy's book' than *The Vanity of Human Wishes* is a boy's poem, or the *Lives of the English Poets* a primer for teenage scribblers.

> Nor where Abassin kings their issue guard,
> Mount Amara, though this by some supposed
> True Paradise, under the Ethiop line
> By Nilus' head, enclosed with shining rock,
> A whole day's journey high . . .
>
> (*Paradise Lost*, Book IV)

It seems that Johnson was the second writer, not the first, to locate the Abyssinian princes' place of confinement in a valley rather than on a mountain, but a valley is apt for his purposes, a position more likely to be 'happy' than a mountain, and more relaxing. Truth or the truths of ordinary life stand on the hills, cragged and steep, outside. The resemblances of the happy valley to the Garden of Eden have been noted; one difference is that Adam and Eve had something to do (who were then the gentlemen?), and had each other. The happy valley is an artificial paradise, a Versailles in exile, and remote from that first and barely imaginable one. Rasselas appears in the guise of the old Adam, if not unregenerated at all events unsatisfied: he is the first who has complained of misery in the happy valley, we are told. 'I can discover within me no power of perception which is not glutted with its proper pleasure, yet I do not feel myself delighted.' He surmises that the happiness of the animals is greater or at least less mixed than that of man, but he has the good sense not to envy their felicity – 'for it is not the felicity of man', whatever that may be and wherever it may reside. He is pleased – we note with amusement – at his own perspicacity in this matter and his own eloquence, like a writer who is elevated by the delicacy with which he has portrayed a lowness of spirits. He calls to mind an Adam in search of a serpent – 'I have already enjoyed too much,' he informs his old instructor, 'give me something to desire' – or reminds us of that related figure, Faust. Though further gone in years, Goethe's hero, too, is oppressed with a nameless pain, exhibits a similar petulance (but one far more literary than Rasselas's), and in a condescending way contrasts his discontent not with the animals but with the simple felicity of the common people celebrating Easter. Rasselas knows nothing of the common people and his terms of reference are much less grand, but it is clear from the outset that his grand tour is to be tinged with irony, direct though not obtrusive, and there will be no epic division or confrontation as between the flatulently aspiring Faust and the deflatorily cynical Mephistopheles.

Rasselas at twenty-six is bright almost to the point of pertness. When the old man tells him that if he had seen the miseries of the world he would know how to value his present condition he retorts that now he has something to desire – to see the miseries of the world, since the sight of them is necessary to happiness. The old man is taken aback at the failure of his tactics; if Johnson saw himself as an instructor of the young, then he viewed himself as such with irony. For the young man is right. He must *see* these miseries, for to see is to share in some degree – 'Life must be seen before it can be known,' Johnson wrote in his 'Review of *A Free Enquiry into the Nature and Origin of Evil*' – and it is not enough for his instructors to *tell* him, as they have done amply, of those miseries. 'All judgment is comparative,' Imlac is to declare in Chapter xxx: 'To judge rightly of the present we must oppose it to the past.' Life, like literature, is understood by reference to the comparisons and contrasts it affords. Even the happy valley – and it can hardly be intensely happy – must depend for its happiness on a degree of unhappiness, however slight: more skilful musicians or dancers coming after less skilful, or subtle monkeys set off by sullen apes, or (just possibly) a stomach at peace after a brief indigestion. We might observe at this point that Imlac's account of the state of affairs in the happy valley in Chapter xii ('It must happen that one will please more than another') makes the inhabitants sound rather like Milton's fallen angels: 'The invitations, by which they allure others to a state which they feel to be wretched, proceed from the natural malignity of hopeless misery . . . They envy the liberty which their folly has forfeited, and would gladly see all mankind imprisoned like themselves.'

Yet the mere idea of unhappiness does afford Rasselas a certain initial happiness, for he spends twenty months daydreaming about the good he could do in the world, 'the relief of distress, the detection of fraud, the defeat of oppression, and the diffusion of happiness'. If children's games are a preparation for later life, then Rasselas's dreaming is the first stage of his growing up, belated no doubt, but praiseworthy in a sequestered princeling whose education has omitted the notion of active benevolence as distinct from an empty pity for 'those whom fate had excluded from this seat of tranquillity'. That he then passes four months, we are told, in resolving to lose no more time in idle resolves is a general reflection on human nature and perhaps a particular one on Johnson's own dilatoriness and unfulfilled literary resolves, 'much intended and little done'.

The inventor of Chapter VI comes to grief, but he is no mere Aunt Sally. 'To swim is to fly in a grosser fluid, and to fly is to swim in a subtler.' Johnson's interest in scientific inquiry and in 'engines' was genuine and informed (that Rasselas himself is no mere pasteboard puppet is shown by Johnson's endowing him with his own pleasure in every kind of knowledge), and the inventor's lecture impresses as all the sounder and more advanced than it would have done not so long ago. He describes the phenomenon of weightlessness and free fall quite expertly, and (though he evades Rasselas's query about breathing difficulties) his forebodings concerning the military use of flight are apropos. Given such sound principles, we are almost surprised that the invention should fail, but its failure may be taken as an acknowledgement that more knowledge is yet required, and not as a condemnation of Faustian presumptuousness or a ridiculing of crankiness. Johnson was no Luddite; in *Adventurer* 99 he had this to say about 'projectors':

That the attempts of such men will often miscarry, we may reasonably expect; yet from such men, and such only, are we to hope for the cultivation of those parts of nature which lie yet waste, and the invention of those arts which are yet wanting to the felicity of life . . . Many that presume to laugh at projectors, would consider a flight through the air in a winged chariot, and the movement of a mighty engine by the steam of water, as equally the dreams of mechanic lunacy . . .

Incidentally, G. B. Hill well illustrated the difference between *Rasselas* and Voltaire's much darker assault on optimism, *Candide* (published a few weeks earlier than *Rasselas* and at that time unread by Johnson), when he said,

'Johnson is content with giving the artist a ducking. Voltaire would have crippled him for life at the very least; most likely would have killed him on the spot.'

We first meet Imlac in Chapter VII when he is reciting a poem 'upon the various conditions of humanity' which catches the prince's attention, and might well be *The Vanity of Human Wishes*, written ten years earlier. Though the author includes his other persons in his intellectual patronage, Imlac speaks for Johnson where the subject of poetry is concerned – if, as we shall see, somewhat ambiguously – and his attitude towards the royal pupil he has acquired (he 'pitied his ignorance, and loved his curiosity') is eminently Johnsonian. So, strikingly, are his remarks on inconsistencies, and on real and unreal wants.

Chapter X has been the most frequently quoted, as a résumé of neo-classical (and specifically Johnsonian) literary theory. 'The business of a poet . . . is to examine, not the individual, but the species; to remark general properties and large appearances: he does not number the streaks of the tulip, or describe the different shades in the verdure of the forest.' Side by side with this we may place a passage from Johnson's *Preface* to his edition of Shakespeare (1765):

Nothing can please many, and please long, but just representations of general nature. Particular manners can be known to few, and therefore few only can judge how nearly they are copied . . . His characters are not modified by the customs of particular places, unpractised by the rest of the world; by the peculiarities of studies or professions, which can operate but upon small numbers; or by the accidents of transient fashions or temporary opinions: they are the genuine progeny of common humanity such as the world will always supply, and observation will always find . . . In the writings of other poets a character is too often an individual; in those of Shakespeare it is commonly a species.

Whatever plea one may enter for streaks and peculiarities and the thisness of one tulip as compared with another (features which modern writing is rich in, often at the cost of a larger poverty, the peculiarities tending to sink to perversions), the fact remains that what Johnson says is true of Shakespeare and must account in large part for the longevity and universality of his reputation. But Imlac goes on, contradicting what he has said and, quite directly, what Johnson said in connection with Shakespeare: the poet 'must be acquainted likewise with all the modes of life', he must 'trace the changes of the human mind as they are modified by various institutions and accidental influences of climate or custom ...' The peculiarities and particular customs seem to have crept back in! Mr Fussell comments that as we listen to Imlac carrying on, we begin to realize that these are the notions less of a poet than of a failed poet. Not necessarily: perhaps it is Dr Johnson, not at present on his best behaviour as a literary panjandrum, who is sending himself up, acknowledging in humorous fashion that literature is too large for any prescriptive theory to cope with at all safely, and that, where poetry is concerned, whether or not inconsistencies cannot all be right, they may all be true. While nothing that Imlac says is arrant nonsense, his ambition to be complete and exhaustive is vain, and Johnson dismisses the ambition lightly and nicely at the beginning of the next chapter. 'Enough!' exclaims the prince, who wants to hear about life: 'Thou hast convinced me, that no human being can ever be a poet.'

First, however, Rasselas is treated to a disquisition (or what the chapter title mischievously calls 'a hint') on pilgrimage. 'Long journeys in search of truth are not commanded,' one can stay at home and be pious: on the other hand, holy places 'may operate upon our own minds in an uncommon manner' – a balanced presentation, in which a severe rationality yields properly to human nature, as in Johnson's comments in *A Journey to the Western Islands of Scotland*:

> Far from me and from my friends, be such frigid philosophy as may conduct us indifferent and unmoved over any ground which has been dignified by wisdom, bravery, or virtue. That man is little to be envied, whose patriotism would not gain force

upon the plain of *Marathon*, or whose piety would not grow warmer among the ruins of *Iona*!

On life itself, Imlac is more taciturn, as if it comprehends the worst aspects of both marriage and celibacy: 'Human life is every where a state in which much is to be endured, and little to be enjoyed.' In the face of this, the prince may be allowed, as corrective, an unrebuked expression of the more gentle, anti-technological side of hippie philosophy: 'I would injure no man ... I would relieve every distress ... why should not life glide quietly away in the soft reciprocation of protection and reverence? All this may be done without the help of European refinements, which appear by their effects to be rather specious than useful.' And despite what Imlac has said about life outside, he tells Rasselas that he doesn't know a single one of the prince's attendants who does not lament the hour when he entered the happy valley. (Presumably Rasselas was only the first to dare to complain aloud.) Now dissatisfaction is out in the open and the prince has a like-minded companion: it only remains to find a means of escape. They are promptly joined by Rasselas's sister, Nekayah ('Permit me to fly with you from this tasteless tranquillity'), and, in a spirit of duty and propriety rather than from free choice, by her favourite maid, Pekuah.

3

In the outside world the prince expects to be obeyed, and the princess that others should prostrate themselves before her: in their beginning, we shall note, is their end. But both are sufficiently adaptable, helped in this by the holiday spirit which prevails (Imlac is really rather fortunate in his pupils), and Johnson pays a little homage to 'realism' by informing us that two years are spent in studying the language of Egypt.

Rasselas's first sight of Cairo is most favourable, up to a point: everybody seems to be happy except, incomprehensibly, himself. To suppose others to be happy, to lack happiness oneself, but to counterfeit the appearance of happiness – this is a common phenomenon, Imlac tells him in a sub-Mephistophelean way, and he should not suppose that fate has picked him out for special treatment. The prince therefore turns from pleasure to wisdom, and is deeply impressed by a high-minded sage: 'I have found . . . a man who can teach all that is necessary to be known . . .' Imlac replies in a manner which would surely discourage the young person seeking a blueprint for life from this work: 'Be not too hasty . . . to trust, or to admire, the teachers of morality: they discourse like angels, but they live like men.' Confirmation follows speedily, for the prince finds the philosopher in deep distress at the death of his only daughter: 'My views, my purposes, my hopes are at an end . . .' Briefly but firmly the prince reproaches him for departing from his own precepts: 'Has wisdom no strength to arm the heart against calamity?' Mr Wiltshire comments that 'our sympathies are all with the crushed old man, and Rasselas's questions, however just, appear callow and heartless'. I think we do read the incident in this way – even though our sympathy for the philosopher is somewhat undermined in advance by his partiality for gold – and we learn something extra to what the prince has learnt about 'the emptiness of rhetorical sound'. Johnson could hardly not be thinking about his mother at this point: he wrote the tale to make money to send her in her last days, and paid for her funeral out of it. While allowing the prince the element of priggishness usual in the young heroes of the *Bildungs-roman*, Johnson seems to endorse the attitude movingly embodied in a poem written by the slightly later Japanese Buddhist, Issa, on the death of his only daughter:

> The world of dew
> Is a world of dew . . . and yet,
> And yet . . .

Sir John Hawkins recorded that, despite Johnson's stoicism, he was 'as little able to sustain the shock' of his mother's death 'as he would have been had this loss befallen him in his nonage'.

The myth that the possession of wisdom can immunize you against the calamities of life ('Dispute it like a man' – we remember Macduff's answer: 'But I must also feel it as a man') having thus been disposed of, we are straightaway directed to another myth and its demolition in 'A Glimpse of pastoral life'. 'This,' says Imlac as they wend their way through fields, flocks and shepherds, 'is the life which has been often celebrated for its innocence and quiet.' But alas, the shepherds are 'rude and ignorant' and discontented, considering themselves 'condemned to labour for the luxury of the rich'. This abrupt dismissal of a class with no doubt some justice in their complaints is alleviated by an ironic picture of the affronted princess persevering none the less in a private myth of herself, neither rude nor ignorant, fondling her lambs and listening, 'without care, among brooks and breezes, to one of her maidens reading in the shade'. It does not seem probable that the author was vitally interested in either the rude shepherds or the princessly shepherdess.

Chapter xx takes us from the resentful poor to the unfortunate rich, and the princess again obliges with a display of sensibility: their wealthy host is envied by the 'Bassa of Egypt' ('My prosperity puts my life in danger'), and grief and indignation so upset her that she retires to her apartment. We have heard about the penalties of wealth in *The Vanity of Human Wishes*:

> How much more safe the vassal than the lord;
> Low skulks the hind beneath the rage of pow'r,
> And leaves the wealthy traitor in the Tow'r,
> Untouch'd his cottage, and his slumbers sound,
> Tho' confiscation's vultures hover round.

But in his less poetic or more judicious moods, Johnson knew that the pains of poverty were a good deal harder to bear. In reviewing Soame Jenyns's *A Free Enquiry into the*

Nature and Origin of Evil, a work which bears the misfortunes of others cheerfully, he quotes the opinion voiced
there (and in Pope's *An Essay on Man*), that 'Poverty . . . is
generally compensated by having more hopes, and fewer
fears', and demolishes it with one powerful and well-aimed
blow:

> The poor indeed are insensible of many little vexations which
> sometimes embitter the possessions and pollute the enjoyments
> of the rich. They are not pained by casual incivility, or mortified
> by the mutilation of a compliment; but this happiness is like that
> of a malefactor, who ceases to feel the cords that bind him when
> the pincers are tearing his flesh.

There follow two short vignettes, the first portraying a
famous hermit who describes how he became disillusioned
successively with the life of a senior army officer, with
mineralogy and botany and with seclusion. He cannot
praise a cloistered virtue, questions his motives for retirement, digs up his treasure, and accompanies his visitors
back to Cairo with every sign of enthusiasm. The second
episode concerns a Rousseau-esque philosopher who
preaches that the recipe for happiness is to live according to
nature. When the prince asks humbly for a definition of the
process he is treated to a splendid sentence of circular
gobbledegook. Neither encounter helps the visitors in their
'choice of life'; the first demonstrates Johnson's gift for
creating an ironic situation without employing any of the
verbal means to irony, while the second is a nimble parodic
manipulation of the kind of large abstractions and general-
ities in which he himself has been accused of excessive indulgence.

The prince and his sister then divide the labour of
observation and research between them: he is to explore
'the splendour of courts', while she investigates 'the shades
of humbler life'. The prince's share is soon completed: he
just has time to convince himself that the all-powerful
Bassa enjoys the 'sublime delight' of ruling over a whole
nation before the Bassa is deposed by his Turkish overlord

and carried off to Constantinople in chains. In case we should delude ourselves that there is a *superior* superiority to be enjoyed on earth, we are told that in turn the Sultan himself is murdered by his janizaries. The princess comes back with rather more material to exercise their minds. She has found little to impress her favourably in domestic life – accustomed to the conversation of Imlac and Rasselas, she finds her coevals vapid prattlers – but a good deal to say about the generation gap and even more about matrimony. Ian White has noted, of the setting of the tale, 'Egypt is not only the country "where the sciences first dawned that illuminate the world", but also that "beyond which the arts cannot be traced of civil society or domestic life".'

The debate on marriage is the most elaborate and sustained in the book, for there is so much to be said on both sides – even though the most famous saying is said early on, by Nekayah: 'Marriage has many pains, but celibacy has no pleasures.' Much good sense is spoken, and if parts of it are irreconcilable with other parts, then irreconcilabilities, though they cannot all be right, must, when imputed to man, all be true. According to Boswell, Johnson maintained that a lawyer had no business with the justice or otherwise of the case in hand, for his function was to deploy art and power in arranging the evidence. Here and elsewhere in *Rasselas* Johnson is arranging the evidence, sometimes the evidence on both sides of the case. Boswell also remarked that Johnson could be 'the greatest sophist that ever contended in the lists of declamation' and in company would often argue on the wrong side 'with equal warmth and ingenuity'. But, Boswell continued, Johnson 'was too conscientious to make error permanent and pernicious by deliberately writing it'. Open-ended as *Rasselas* is – within, we are bound to add, its sombre frontiers – at no point is any view which Johnson would consider immoral given any sort of force or appeal.

Marriage, the prince proposes, is one of the means of happiness. The princess, whose sensibility must have been

sorely wounded by her researches, makes the counter-
proposition that marriage is one of 'the innumerable modes
of human misery'. Rasselas reminds her that she has represented celibacy as less happy than marriage, and 'both conditions may be bad, but they cannot both be worst'. It all
depends, is roughly what Nekayah counters with, or (as
Rambler 63 puts it): 'To take a view at once distinct and
comprehensive of human life, with all its intricacies of
combination, and varieties of connexion, is beyond the
power of mortal intelligences.' For a moment a tiff
threatens to break out, a mild demonstration perhaps of
how easily domestic harmony is imperilled. However, the
disputants, who seem to have advanced considerably in the
processes of logical argument, go on to prove quite satis-
factorily that late marriage is preferable to early marriage
(the partners will be more mature in judgement, less driven
by blind desire and visibly older than their children, with
whom therefore they will not find themselves competing)
and also that early marriage is preferable to late marriage
(opinions will be less fixed and habits less ingrained, the
partners will be more flexible and they will be able to super-
vise the growing up of their children). Rasselas finally
wonders whether there may not be an optimum age for
marriage, neither too early nor too late, but to the princess
this suggests (though not in such crude terms) the donkey
who starves to death between two equidistant carrots.
Something has to be chosen, and something surrendered.
'No man,' she says in an apter metaphor, 'can, at the same
time, fill his cup from the source and from the mouth of the
Nile.'

The space devoted to this attempt to establish the best
time of life for marrying, however inconclusive the
attempt, at least implies that marriage has the edge over
celibacy, by and large: that in fact, in Nekayah's prelimin-
ary summing-up, 'Marriage has many pains, but celibacy
has no pleasures,' the 'but' has more than the neutral con-
junctive value of 'and'. We are not too sorry that Imlac
now enters and changes the subject: 'It seems to me ...

that while you are making the choice of life, you neglect to live.'

4

Imlac's seemingly odd way of repairing this defect – Rasselas and Nekayah find it odd – is to take them to see the pyramids. He points out that 'to judge rightly of the present we must oppose it to the past' and that, whether for private persons or for public, history is a necessary study. 'Ignorance,' he informs them in stern tones and characteristically Johnsonian mode, 'when it is voluntary, is criminal.' In fact, the visit serves two important purposes. Unlike its rival, the Great Wall of China, the Great Pyramid in itself serves no useful purpose commensurate with its expense.

It seems to have been erected only in compliance with that hunger of imagination which preys incessantly upon life, and must be always appeased by some employment. Those who have already all that they can enjoy, must enlarge their desires ... I consider this mighty structure as a monument of the insufficiency of human enjoyments.

We may feel that, as a dreadful warning, the pyramid is less effective than the trunkless legs and shattered visage of Shelley's Ozymandias, king of kings. The pyramid stands at least and, however inexplicably, it does impress the visitors – as it must do if Imlac is to hang an important and strongly felt moral tale thereby. But no admonitory reflection on the transitoriness of worldly glory and power is intended. The theme is man's continuing dissatisfaction, his hunger for the new, the phenomenon which Faust prided himself on as a sign of a superior nature –

> When phantoms haunt him, let him go his way:
> In onward-striding finding pain and joy,
> He, every moment uncontented ...

– and which Imlac registers sadly as a central fact of the human condition, to be accepted perforce but not glorified, affecting mere men as well as kings of kings. The difference is that Faust believes that discontent drives out boredom by transforming itself into aspiration or 'onward-striding', whereas Imlac sees it as leading, with but a short respite, from boredom back to boredom. I would guess that, when it came to estimating the possibility of supplying 'the appetite of novelty' with an adequate and legitimate provision of 'perpetual gratifications', the two authors, Goethe and Johnson, would find themselves in substantial agreement. They both stood roughly equidistant (though it took Goethe longer to get there) from the two extremes of sanguineness and cynicism.

The second purpose served by the visit is that, as Frederick W. Hilles has put it, 'the observers become participants': the party is thrown into personal distress by the abduction of Pekuah, a happening which testifies to Mr Hilles's comment that *Rasselas* is filled with 'psychological insights developed through irony'. For Pekuah was kidnapped because she thought it safer to stay outside than to enter the pyramid: she could have been right, but as it happened she was wrong, and another wish has proved vain. Though the princess is inconsolable, Imlac contrives to lessen her self-reproach. Nekayah argues that she should not have indulged Pekuah in her fears – 'She ought to have feared me more than spectres': that is not exactly self-reproach, though it is a nice touch – but Imlac tells her that she should not blame herself for what was well and kindly intended. How much worse it would be if Pekuah had been carried off because the princess had obliged her to stay outside, or if the princess had forced her to enter the pyramid and the poor girl had 'died before you in agonies of terrour'! The conspectus of possibilities is managed nimbly – it was noted by his acquaintances that Johnson's mind resembled an elephant's trunk, 'strong to buffet even the tiger, and pliable to pick up even the pin' – and with humaneness.

It is perhaps true that Pekuah absent is treasured more highly by the princess than was Pekuah present: she is now well-nigh canonized. But Johnson casts no ironic doubt on the genuineness and depth of Nekayah's sorrow. Imlac's solacing is sympathetic and just: 'Our minds, like our bodies, are in continual flux; something is hourly lost, and something acquired ... Do not suffer life to stagnate; it will grow muddy for want of motion: commit yourself again to the current of the world ...' In fact, the princess continues to grieve for her maid until Pekuah is restored – between nine months and a year later – and, while the demands of life intervene along with its 'common cares and common pleasures', Johnson tells us quite simply that 'her real love of Pekuah was yet not diminished'. Moreover, she has learnt that 'happiness itself is the cause of misery', for only that which is truly loved can be sorely missed.

Voltaire's Cunégonde suffered very considerable indignities and *la vieille* was not only raped but deprived of part of her buttocks. Pekuah's experiences as a victim of abduction are in a different class, and she gains much by them. (In passing we may note that when exhorting her to pull herself together and enter the pyramid, Nekayah told her: 'Remember that you are the companion of the princess of Abissinia'; before long, when they call upon the astronomer, Pekuah will be the leader and the princess her undesignated companion or chaperon.) Not only was she taken for herself a princess, but the Arab chief, her captor, turned out to be a gentleman ('I know the rules of civil life'), even something of a philosopher. 'The angels of affliction,' he tells her in complimentary vein, 'spread their toils alike for the virtuous and the wicked, for the mighty and the mean.' Furthermore, Pekuah is relieved to find, 'his predominant passion was desire of money', and she knows that avarice is 'an uniform and tractable vice', in this view not differing much from Johnson, whom Boswell reported as saying, 'There are few ways in which a man can be more innocently employed than in getting money.' Pekuah's opinion of life in the harem is much like Nekayah's opinion of the daughters of the middle classes: it was not surprising, she tells the company on her return, that the Arab could find little solid pleasure in the society of his women, pretty though they might be ('ignoble beauty' is her phrase), and derive small pride from their 'fondness', since they had no 'choice'. For intellectual pleasure he turned to Pekuah, we gather, or her maids, relatively emancipated females. Her only fear was that admiration might turn to inconvenient love, but happily gold won the day over both the Arab's intellectual inclinations and his amorous aspirations.

The prince has decided to devote himself to science, and so, Imlac feels, another cautionary example is required. This is provided by the learned astronomer of Chapter XL, who combines profundity of mind, integrity and ready benevolence – 'Surely this man is happy,' says the princess – with madness. The astronomer has revealed his little difficulty to Imlac: for the past five years he has regulated the world's weather and distributed the seasons, administering this 'great office' with 'exact justice'. We observe that the progress from observing and predicting to believing that one is commanding and creating is sufficiently comprehensible, containing the element of 'logic' which characterizes all forms of madness, as distinct from idiocy. The astronomer's troubles are threefold: occasionally he suspects he is mad (the least of his distresses); he cannot prove by external evidence that he regulates the weather (as a scientist he knows the importance of 'the laws of demonstration'), and he is agitated by the necessity of finding a suitable successor to himself (obviously the post calls for considerable strength and purity of character).

Comic as this episode promises to be, there ensues a sombre and moving study of madness, not as a special and rare condition afflicting a particularly formed or deformed class of persons but as something which is never far away from any of us. 'Few can attain this man's knowledge, and few practise his virtues; but all may suffer his calamity. Of the uncertainties of our present state, the most dreadful and alarming is the uncertain continuance of reason.' Imlac traces the development of madness: the hungry imagination gets the better of reason (the more readily in those who are too much alone and given to speculation, though perhaps, 'if we speak with rigorous exactness, no human mind is in its right state'); fancy 'grows first imperious, and in time despotick', and 'fictions begin to operate as realities' – the sufferer has been imperceptibly but firmly taken over by an obsession. Intelligence, learning and nobility of character are no defence, for, though he has come to think that in some way alarming to himself he is God, the astronomer is a true humanist.

The only possible cure for the astronomer's disease is to bring him into human society. He is not normally accessible to female visitors unless they are in distress (and to pose as such, Rasselas points out, would be to forfeit the astronomer's confidence), but happily the apprenticeship which Pekuah has served under her Arab captor enables her to arouse the astronomer's curiosity and secures their admission. Pekuah has grown in stature during the tale, perhaps more noticeably than the others, and her conversation soon 'took possession of his heart'. The astronomer is invited frequently to Imlac's house, 'where they distinguished him by extraordinary respect' (we may be forgiven for thinking of Johnson's reception into the Thrale family), and he begins to 'delight in sublunary pleasures' – a beautifully apt adjective. Though his condition is exacerbated by guilt arising out of his newly found peace, he achieves to some extent the advice Imlac offered to the princess distraught at the loss of Pekuah, he is again committed to the current of the world. First Pekuah and then, as Imlac tells him, his own learning and virtue give him hopes of a more certain peace of mind.

J. P. Hardy has called this episode 'climactic'. It is hard to say whether anything in *Rasselas* is more climactic, or more central, than anything else, such is the work's solidity and economy, but undeniably the subject of the episode is one which affected Johnson himself with personal immediacy, strongly and fearfully. So much is clear from the persuasive subtlety of the diagnosis, the absence of irony (though not altogether of humour), and the feeling gravity of tone. A count might show that the word most frequently recurrent in *Rasselas* is 'terrour'. (Possibly it would share first place with 'inquire'.)

The meeting with the old man which has interceded – serving to separate Imlac's 'history' of the astronomer from their actual meeting with him – adds little to the more cheerful part of the account of old age given in *The Vanity of Human Wishes* (ll. 289–308), but it directs our attention to the better happiness and greater virtue to be looked for after death. The company go on to discuss the monastic life, a topic arising out of Rasselas's remark that variety is necessary to content, and Imlac lists its advantages: 'Whatever is done by the monks is incited by an adequate and reasonable motive.' Yet 'he that lives well in the world is better than he that lives well in a monastery': it is a sign of Johnson's disinclination to sacrifice exhaustiveness (and in this case compassion) for the sake of a strong and compact epigram that Imlac continues, 'But, perhaps, every one is not able to stem the temptations of publick life', and there are the weary, the sick and the timorous to take into the account. Moreover, though not virtuous in itself, mortification 'disengages us from the allurements of sense' and prepares us for the end of our present state and the beginning of our next.

Rasselas is unenthusiastic when it is proposed that they should pay a visit to the catacombs – Johnson has all along allowed that, within limits, attitudes quite properly differ at different stages of life and that what is appropriate to age is not necessarily so to youth – but agrees to 'do' the catacombs on the grounds that he wants to do something. A nice touch of easy and natural humour occurs when Pekuah insists, this time, on entering 'the habitations of the dead'. Once they are there, they engage in a brisk bout of hard philosophizing, philosophizing of a professional character, on the immateriality of the soul, with Imlac, on a more elevated level and in reverse, doing what Johnson himself did in kicking a large stone to refute Berkeley's subjective idealism. 'All the conclusions of reason enforce the immateriality of mind, and all the notices of sense and investigations of science concur to prove the unconsciousness of matter.' The princess has the last word: 'To me . . . the choice of life is become less important; I hope hereafter to think only on the choice of eternity.'

5

Chapter XLIX brings the conclusion 'in which nothing is concluded'. Confined to the house by the rising of the Nile, they divert themselves with talk of 'various schemes of happiness which each of them had formed'. Pekuah wishes to be prioress of a convent, the princess to found a college for women 'in which she would preside', the prince desires 'a little kingdom, in which he might administer justice in his own person, and see all the parts of government with his own eyes', but, we are told, 'he could never fix the limits of his dominion, and was always adding to the number of his subjects'. Critics have detected more irony in Johnson's account of these wishes than probably exists. The three wishes, Mr Fussell says, are ironic not only in that they cannot possibly be fulfilled but also because they betray a 'secret lust for power over others', each of the wishers assuming that he or she will be top dog. Moreover, Mr Fussell holds that the norm, against which the young people's ambitions are to be seen as 'both vain and corrupt', is established by the contentment of Imlac and the astronomer 'to be driven along the stream of life without directing their course to any particular port'. In answer to this reading we must surely remark that what is right for the elderly is not right for the young, and Rasselas, Nekayah and Pekuah have life substantially in front of them. And we shall ask whether their wishes are either so 'corrupt' or so utterly impossible of attainment.

Our young people have shown themselves more than usually intelligent, competent and decent, and they have learnt much. It is not conceivable that, at the end of a journey on which he has plainly enjoyed their company, the author would impute folly and corruptness to them, however indirectly. There is certainly nothing shameful in their ambitions. Johnson would not deny that someone has to be in charge, and the better the top dog, the better the lot of the underdogs. Rasselas would in fact make a good king, Nekayah a good college principal, and Pekuah a good prioress – though in view of the princess's piety and her favourite's blue stockings one can perhaps envisage the two exchanging their roles to some advantage. Whatever ironic pressure has been brought to bear upon the phrase 'the choice of life' – Johnson's original title for the work – and whatever dominion must be allowed to chance, that 'subtle and insidious power' (it is chance that has made Rasselas a prince), the fact remains that on occasion choice not only can be made but must be:

No course of life is so prescribed and limited, but that many actions must result from arbitrary election. Every one must form the general plan of his conduct by his own reflections; he must resolve whether he will endeavour at riches or at content; whether he will exercise private or publick virtues; whether he will labour for the general benefit of mankind, or contract his beneficence to his family and dependants.

(*Rambler* 184)

Elsewhere Johnson remarked, reasonably enough, that not too much of life should be spent in deliberating how to spend it.

What lends feasibility to the view of Mr Fussell and others is of course the author's comment, in the penultimate sentence of the book, 'Of these wishes that they had formed they well knew that none could be obtained' – though it is worth observing that the sentence also serves to exculpate them of folly and corruptness. Not many words have been wasted in *Rasselas*, but here Johnson is laconic by his own standards, and I remain unconvinced that the meaning of his comment has been wholly taken. Read as an indicator to the silliness or corruptness of their ambitions, if it really can be read thus, it surely runs

counter to the book itself. It may well be that when Johnson says that none of their wishes could be attained, he has
in mind not the activities themselves but the happiness
which they expect (at the time of naming them) to accompany them. Not all of Pekuah's maidens would be pious,
nor life as a prioress inevitably an 'unvariable state'; the
princess would not invariably succeed in turning her pupils
into 'models of prudence, and patterns of piety'; nor is it
likely that Rasselas could administer total justice in his own
person to the totality of his subjects, whatever their number: indeed, in Chapter xxvii, 'Disquisition upon greatness', he asserted quite explicitly the impossibility of this
ever happening. Top dogs are not exempt from the human
condition: good kings, good prioresses, good college prin-
cipals, all are exposed to the disappointments, the reversals,
the trials and tribulations, and the boredom which the book
has told us about. 'Sir, sorrow is inherent in humanity.'
But that is another matter.

They resolve to return to Abyssinia, where they will
certainly do something – but not to the happy valley, where
they would do nothing, for that is impossible to conceive
of. 'He who does his best, however little, is always to be
distinguished from him who does nothing,' Johnson wrote
in *Rambler* 177. That is not to say very much, and perhaps
we must set against it this passage from *A Journey to the
Western Islands of Scotland* – it arises, quasi-apologetically,
out of Johnson's 'undignified' comments on the incom-
modious windows and inadequate ventilation of Scottish
houses:

... it must be remembered, that life consists not of a series of
illustrious actions, or elegant enjoyments; the greater part of our
time passes in compliance with necessities, in the performance of
daily duties, in the removal of small inconveniencies, in the
procurement of petty pleasures ...

True, but Rasselas is a prince – in Chapter xvi he remarked, unreproved by Imlac, on the advantage his birth
had given him – and can in fact look forward to 'illustrious

actions', and Nekayah is a princess. (And Pekuah is at least clever, cultivated, charming and well connected.) True also, but Johnson was not writing for princes and princesses, and since he was writing for and about man at large, concerned with the species, its general properties, and not with the aristocratic streaks, he may have felt obliged to pour some cold water on those individual and rather grand wishes. One thing is certain, of the conclusion as of the rest of the book, and Joseph Wood Krutch has expressed it well: Johnson has done 'something more than merely rephrase the commonplaces which have long served to demonstrate that all is vanity', for his pessimism 'was not merely of that vulgar sort which is no more than a lament over the failure of worldly prosperity. It was, instead, the pessimism which is more properly called the tragic sense of life . . .' There is no malignancy or other deforming animus in his irony, and, as A. R. Humphreys has said, it 'never indicates on Johnson's part any self-congratulation on superior wisdom'.

Another quotation, from Matthew Hodgart, if we enter the Imlacian proviso that the past is never dead so long as there is a present, may serve to end this introduction:

In many of his opinions and prejudices, religious, political, or critical, Johnson belongs to the dead past; in his tolerance, energy, and intelligence he belongs to a world which is still possible.

D. J. ENRIGHT

NOTE ON THE TEXT

The present text is based upon the second edition of
Rasselas (2 volumes, 1759) as revised by Johnson and published two months after the first edition (also in 2 volumes).
It includes the minor verbal changes made by the author in
the second edition, but reverts to the first edition in some
details of spelling and punctuation where new printing
errors have occurred in the second. The spelling has not
been modernized on principle, but when a word occurs in
two different forms (e.g. 'persue' and 'pursue', 'mon-
astry' and 'monastery'), and no benefit derives from the
inconsistency, I have adopted the modern form.

D.J.E.

SELECT BIBLIOGRAPHY

G. B. HILL, ed., *The History of Rasselas, Prince of Abissinia*, Clarendon Press, Oxford, 1887.

R. W. CHAPMAN, ed., *The History of Rasselas, Prince of Abissinia*, Clarendon Press, Oxford, 1927.

J. P. HARDY, ed., *The History of Rasselas, Prince of Abissinia*, Oxford University Press, London, 1968.

GEOFFREY TILLOTSON and BRIAN JENKINS, eds, *The History of Rasselas, Prince of Abissinia*, Oxford University Press, London, 1971.

JOSEPH WOOD KRUTCH, *Samuel Johnson*, New York, 1944; London, 1948 [new edition, Harcourt Brace, 1963].

G. J. KOLB, 'The Structure of *Rasselas*', *Publications of the Modern Language Association of America*, lxvi, 1951.

F. R. LEAVIS, 'Johnson and Augustanism', *The Common Pursuit*, Chatto & Windus, 1952.

W. J. BATE, *The Achievement of Samuel Johnson*, Oxford University Press, New York, 1955.

A. R. HUMPHREYS, 'Johnson', *From Dryden to Johnson (Pelican Guide to English Literature*, 4), Penguin, 1957.

MATTHEW HODGART, *Samuel Johnson and his Times*, Batsford, 1962.

FREDERICK W. HILLES, '*Rasselas*, An "Uninstructive Tale"', *Johnson, Boswell and Their Circle; Essays Presented to L. F. Powell*, Clarendon Press, Oxford, 1965.

JOHN WILTSHIRE, 'Dr Johnson's Seriousness', *Melbourne Critical Review*, x, 1967.

W. K. WIMSATT, 'In Praise of *Rasselas*', *Imagined Worlds; Essays in Honour of John Butt* (Maynard Mack and Ian Gregor, eds), Methuen, 1968.

PAUL FUSSELL, *Samuel Johnson and the Life of Writing*, Harcourt Brace, New York, 1971; Chatto & Windus, 1972.

IAN WHITE, 'On *Rasselas*', *Cambridge Quarterly*, vi, 1, 1972.

JOHN WAIN, *Samuel Johnson*, Macmillan, 1974.

Facsimile of the titlepage of the first edition, published in 1759

THE
PRINCE
OF
ABISSINIA.

A
TALE.

IN TWO VOLUMES.

VOL. I.

LONDON:

Printed for R. and J. DODSLEY, in Pall-Mall;
and W. JOHNSTON, in Ludgate-Street.
MDCCLIX.

CHAPTER I

Description of a palace in a valley

YE who listen with credulity to the whispers of fancy, and pursue with eagerness the phantoms of hope;[1] who expect that age will perform the promises of youth, and that the deficiencies of the present day will be supplied by the morrow; attend to the history of Rasselas[2] prince of Abissinia.

Rasselas was the fourth son of the mighty emperour, in whose dominions the Father of waters begins his course;[3] whose bounty pours down the streams of plenty, and scatters over half the world the harvests of Egypt.

According to the custom which has descended from age to age among the monarchs of the torrid zone, Rasselas was confined in a private palace, with the other sons and daughters of Abissinian royalty, till the order of succession should call him to the throne.

The place, which the wisdom or policy of antiquity had destined for the residence of the Abissinian princes, was a spacious valley in the kingdom of Amhara, surrounded on every side by mountains, of which the summits overhang the middle part. The only passage, by which it could be entered, was a cavern that passed under a rock, of which it has long been disputed whether it was the work of nature or of human industry. The outlet of the cavern was concealed by a thick wood, and the mouth which opened into the valley was closed with gates of iron, forged by the artificers of ancient days, so massy[4] that no man could, without the help of engines,[5] open or shut them.

From the mountains on every side, rivulets descended that filled all the valley with verdure and fertility, and formed a lake in the middle inhabited by fish of every species, and frequented by every fowl whom nature has taught to dip the wing in water. This lake discharged its superfluities by a stream which entered a dark cleft of the mountain on the northern side, and fell with dreadful noise from precipice to precipice till it was heard no more.

The sides of the mountains were covered with trees, the banks of the brooks were diversified with flowers; every blast shook spices from the rocks, and every month dropped fruits upon the ground. All animals that bite the grass, or brouse the shrub, whether wild or tame, wandered in this extensive circuit, secured from beasts of prey by the mountains which confined them.[6] On one part were flocks and herds feeding in the pastures, on another all the beasts of chase frisking in the lawns; the spritely kid was bounding on the rocks, the subtle monkey frolicking in the trees, and the solemn elephant reposing in the shade. All the diversities of the world were brought together, the blessings of nature were collected, and its evils extracted and excluded.

The valley, wide and fruitful, supplied its inhabitants with the necessaries of life, and all delights and superfluities were added at the annual visit which the emperour paid his children, when the iron gate was opened to the sound of musick; and during eight days every one that resided in the valley was required to propose whatever might contribute to make seclusion pleasant, to fill up the vacancies of attention, and lessen the tediousness of time. Every desire was immediately granted. All the artificers of pleasure were called to gladden the festivity; the musicians exerted the power of harmony, and the dancers showed their activity before the princes, in hope that they should pass their lives in this blissful captivity, to which these only were admitted whose performance was thought able to add novelty to luxury. Such was the appearance of security and delight which this retirement afforded, that they to whom it was new always desired that it might be perpetual; and as those, on whom the iron gate had once closed, were never suffered to return, the effect of longer experience could not be known. Thus every year produced new schemes of delight, and new competitors for imprisonment.

The palace stood on an eminence raised about thirty

paces above the surface of the lake. It was divided into many squares or courts, built with greater or less magnificence according to the rank of those for whom they were designed. The roofs were turned into arches of massy stone joined with a cement that grew harder by time, and the building stood from century to century, deriding the solstitial rains and equinoctial hurricanes, without need of reparation.

This house, which was so large as to be fully known to none but some ancient officers who successively inherited the secrets of the place, was built as if suspicion herself had dictated the plan. To every room there was an open and secret passage, every square had a communication with the rest, either from the upper stories by private galleries, or by subterranean passages from the lower apartments. Many of the columns had unsuspected cavities, in which a long race of monarchs had reposited their treasures. They then closed up the opening with marble, which was never to be removed but in the utmost exigencies of the kingdom; and recorded their accumulations in a book which was itself concealed in a tower not entered but by the emperour, attended by the prince who stood next in succession.

CHAPTER II

The discontent of Rasselas in the happy valley

HERE the sons and daughters of Abissinia[7] lived only to know the soft vicissitudes of pleasure and repose, attended by all that were skilful to delight, and gratified with whatever the senses can enjoy. They wandered in gardens of fragrance, and slept in the fortresses of security. Every art was practised to make them pleased with their own condition. The sages who instructed them, told them of nothing but the miseries of publick life,[8] and described all beyond the mountains as regions of calamity, where discord was always raging, and where man preyed upon man.

To heighten their opinion of their own felicity, they were

daily entertained with songs, the subject of which was the *happy valley*. Their appetites were excited by frequent enumerations of different enjoyments, and revelry and merriment was the business of every hour from the dawn of morning to the close of even.

These methods were generally successful; few of the Princes had ever wished to enlarge their bounds, but passed their lives in full conviction that they had all within their reach that art or nature could bestow, and pitied those whom fate had excluded from this seat of tranquillity, as the sport of chance, and the slaves of misery.

Thus they rose in the morning, and lay down at night, pleased with each other and with themselves, all but Rasselas, who, in the twenty-sixth year of his age, began to withdraw himself from their pastimes and assemblies, and to delight in solitary walks and silent meditation. He often sat before tables covered with luxury, and forgot to taste the dainties that were placed before him: he rose abruptly in the midst of the song, and hastily retired beyond the sound of musick. His attendants observed the change and endeavoured to renew his love of pleasure: he neglected[9] their officiousness,[10] repulsed their invitations, and spent day after day on the banks of rivulets sheltered with trees, where he sometimes listened to the birds in the branches, sometimes observed the fish playing in the stream, and anon[11] cast his eyes upon the pastures and mountains filled with animals, of which some were biting the herbage, and some sleeping among the bushes.

This singularity of his humour made him much observed. One of the Sages, in whose conversation he had formerly delighted, followed him secretly, in hope of discovering the cause of his disquiet. Rasselas, who knew not that any one was near him, having for some time fixed his eyes upon the goats that were brousing among the rocks, began to compare their condition with his own.

'What, said he, makes the difference between man and all the rest of the animal creation? Every beast that strays beside me has the same corporal necessities with myself; he is hungry and crops the grass, he is thirsty and drinks the stream, his thirst and hunger are appeased, he is satisfied and sleeps; he rises again and is hungry, he is again fed and is at rest. I am hungry and thirsty like him, but when thirst and hunger cease I am not at rest; I am, like him, pained with want, but am not, like him, satisfied with fulness. The intermediate hours are tedious and gloomy; I long again to be hungry that I may again quicken my attention. The birds peck the berries or the corn, and fly away to the groves where they sit in seeming happiness on the branches, and waste their lives in tuning one unvaried series of sounds. I likewise can call the lutanist and the singer, but the sounds that pleased me yesterday weary me to day, and will grow yet more wearisome to morrow. I can discover within me no power of perception which is not glutted with its proper[12] pleasure, yet I do not feel myself delighted. Man has surely some latent sense for which this place affords no gratification, or he has some desires distinct from sense which must be satisfied before he can be happy.'

After this he lifted up his head, and seeing the moon rising, walked towards the palace. As he passed through the fields, and saw the animals around him, 'Ye, said he, are happy, and need not envy me that walk thus among you, burthened with myself; nor do I, ye gentle beings, envy your felicity; for it is not the felicity of man. I have many distresses from which ye are free; I fear pain when I do not feel it; I sometimes shrink at evils recollected, and sometimes start at evils anticipated: surely the equity of providence has balanced peculiar sufferings with peculiar enjoyments.'

With observations like these the prince amused himself as he returned, uttering them with a plaintive voice, yet with a look that discovered[13] him to feel some complacence in his own perspicacity, and to receive some solace of the miseries of life, from consciousness of the delicacy with which he felt, and the eloquence with which he bewailed them. He mingled cheerfully in the diversions of the evening, and all rejoiced to find that his heart was lightened.

CHAPTER III

The wants of him that wants nothing

ON the next day his old instructor, imagining that he had
now made himself acquainted with his disease of mind, was
in hope of curing it by counsel, and officiously sought an
opportunity of conference, which the prince, having long
considered him as one whose intellects[14] were exhausted,
was not very willing to afford: 'Why, said he, does this man
thus intrude upon me; shall I be never suffered to forget
those lectures which pleased only while they were new, and
to become new again must be forgotten?' He then walked
into the wood, and composed himself to his usual meditations; when, before his thoughts had taken any settled
form, he perceived his pursuer at his side, and was at first
prompted by his impatience to go hastily away; but, being
unwilling to offend a man whom he had once reverenced
and still loved, he invited him to sit down with him on the
bank.

The old man, thus encouraged, began to lament the
change which had been lately observed in the prince, and to
inquire why he so often retired from the pleasures of the
palace, to loneliness[15] and silence. 'I fly from pleasure, said
the prince, because pleasure has ceased to please; I am
lonely because I am miserable, and am unwilling to cloud
with my presence the happiness of others.' 'You, Sir, said
the sage, are the first who has complained of misery in the
happy valley. I hope to convince you that your complaints
have no real cause. You are here in full possession of all
that the emperour of Abissinia can bestow; here is neither
labour to be endured nor danger to be dreaded, yet here is
all that labour or danger can procure or purchase. Look
round and tell me which of your wants is without supply:
if you want nothing, how are you unhappy?'

'That I want nothing, said the prince, or that I know not

what I want, is the cause of my complaint; if I had any known want, I should have a certain wish; that wish would excite endeavour, and I should not then repine to see the sun move so slowly towards the western mountain, or lament when the day breaks and sleep will no longer hide me from myself. When I see the kids and the lambs chasing one another, I fancy that I should be happy if I had something to pursue. But, possessing all that I can want, I find one day and one hour exactly like another, except that the latter is still more tedious than the former. Let your experience inform me how the day may now seem as short as in my childhood, while nature was yet fresh, and every moment showed me what I never had observed before. I have already enjoyed too much; give me something to desire.'

The old man was surprised at this new species of affliction, and knew not what to reply, yet was unwilling to be silent. 'Sir, said he, if you had seen the miseries of the world, you would know how to value your present state.' 'Now, said the prince, you have given me something to desire; I shall long to see the miseries of the world, since the sight of them is necessary to happiness.'

CHAPTER IV

The prince continues to grieve and muse

AT this time the sound of musick proclaimed the hour of repast, and the conversation was concluded. The old man went away sufficiently discontented to find that his reasonings had produced the only conclusion which they were intended to prevent. But in the decline of life shame and grief are of short duration; whether it be that we bear easily what we have born long, or that, finding ourselves in age less regarded, we less regard others; or, that we look with slight regard upon afflictions, to which we know that the hand of death is about to put an end.

The prince, whose views were extended to a wider space, could not speedily quiet his emotions. He had been before terrified at the length of life which nature promised him, because he considered that in a long time much must be endured; he now rejoiced in his youth, because in many years much might be done.

This first beam of hope, that had been ever darted into his mind, rekindled youth in his cheeks, and doubled the lustre of his eyes. He was fired with the desire of doing something, though he knew not yet with distinctness, either end or means.

He was now no longer gloomy and unsocial; but, considering himself as master of a secret stock of happiness, which he could enjoy only by concealing it, he affected to be busy in all schemes of diversion, and endeavoured to make others pleased with the state of which he himself was weary. But pleasures never can be so multiplied or continued, as not to leave much of life unemployed; there were many hours, both of the night and day, which he could spend without suspicion in solitary thought. The load of life was much lightened: he went eagerly into the assemblies, because he supposed the frequency of his presence necessary to the success of his purposes; he retired gladly to privacy, because he had now a subject of thought.

His chief amusement was to picture to himself that world which he had never seen; to place himself in various conditions; to be entangled in imaginary difficulties, and to be engaged in wild adventures: but his benevolence always terminated his projects in the relief of distress, the detection of fraud, the defeat of oppression, and the diffusion of happiness.

Thus passed twenty months of the life of Rasselas. He busied himself so intensely in visionary bustle, that he forgot his real solitude; and, amidst hourly preparations for the various incidents of human affairs, neglected to consider by what means he should mingle with mankind.

One day, as he was sitting on a bank, he feigned to himself an orphan virgin robbed of her little portion by a treacherous lover, and crying after him for restitution and redress. So strongly was the image impressed upon his mind, that he started up in the maid's defence, and run forward to seize the plunderer with all the eagerness of real pursuit. Fear naturally quickens the flight of guilt. Rasselas could not catch the fugitive with his utmost efforts; but, resolving to weary, by perseverance, him whom he could not surpass in speed, he pressed on till the foot of the mountain stopped his course.

Here he recollected himself, and smiled at his own use-less impetuosity. Then raising his eyes to the mountain, 'This, said he, is the fatal obstacle that hinders at once the enjoyment of pleasure, and the exercise of virtue. How long is it that my hopes and wishes have flown beyond this boundary of my life, which yet I never have attempted to surmount!'

Struck with this reflection, he sat down to muse, and remembered, that since he first resolved to escape from his confinement, the sun had passed twice over him in his annual course. He now felt a degree of regret with which he had never been before acquainted. He considered how much might have been done in the time which had passed, and left nothing real behind it. He compared twenty months with the life of man. 'In life, said he, is not to be counted the ignorance of infancy, or imbecility of age. We are long before we are able to think, and we soon cease from the power of acting. The true period of human existence may be reasonably estimated as forty years, of which I have mused away the four and twentieth part. What I have lost was certain, for I have certainly possessed it; but of twenty months to come who can assure me?'

The consciousness of his own folly pierced him deeply, and he was long before he could be reconciled to himself. 'The rest of my time, said he, has been lost by the crime or folly of my ancestors, and the absurd institutions of my country; I remember it with disgust, yet without remorse: but the months that have passed since new light darted into my soul, since I formed a scheme of reasonable felicity, have been squandered by my own fault. I have lost that which can never be restored: I have seen the sun rise and set for twenty months, an idle gazer on the light of heaven: In this time the birds have left the nest of their mother, and committed themselves to the woods and to the skies: the kid has forsaken the teat, and learned by degrees to climb the rocks in quest of independant sustenance. I only have made no advances, but am still helpless and ignorant. The moon, by more than twenty changes, admonished me of the flux of life; the stream that rolled before my feet upbraided my inactivity. I sat feasting on intellectual luxury,[16] regardless alike of the examples of the earth, and the instructions of the planets. Twenty months are past, who shall restore them!'

These sorrowful meditations fastened upon his mind; he past four months in resolving to lose no more time in idle resolves, and was awakened to more vigorous exertion by hearing a maid, who had broken a porcelain cup, remark, that what cannot be repaired is not to be regretted.

This was obvious; and Rasselas reproached himself that he had not discovered it, having not known, or not considered, how many useful hints are obtained by chance, and how often the mind, hurried by her own ardour to distant views, neglects the truths that lie open before her. He, for a few hours, regretted his regret, and from that time bent his whole mind upon the means of escaping from the valley of happiness.

CHAPTER V

The prince meditates his escape

HE now found that it would be very difficult to effect that which it was very easy to suppose effected. When he looked round about him, he saw himself confined by the bars of nature which had never yet been broken, and by the gate, through which none that once had passed it were ever able to return. He was now impatient as an eagle in a grate.[17] He passed week after week in clambering the mountains, to see if there was any aperture which the bushes might conceal, but found all the summits inaccessible by their prominence.[18] The iron gate he despaired to open; for it was not only secured with all the power of art, but was always watched by successive sentinels, and was by its position exposed to the perpetual observation of all the inhabitants.

He then examined the cavern through which the waters of the lake were discharged; and, looking down at a time when the sun shone strongly upon its mouth, he discovered it to be full of broken rocks, which, though they permitted the stream to flow through many narrow passages, would stop any body of solid bulk. He returned discouraged and dejected; but, having now known the blessing of hope, resolved never to despair.

In these fruitless searches he spent ten months. The time, however, passed cheerfully away: in the morning he rose with new hope, in the evening applauded his own diligence, and in the night slept sound after his fatigue. He met a thousand amusements which beguiled his labour, and diversified his thoughts. He discerned the various instincts of animals, and properties of plants, and found the place replete with wonders, of which he purposed to solace himself with the contemplation, if he should never be able to accomplish his flight; rejoicing that his endeavours, though yet unsuccessful, had supplied him with a source of inexhaustible inquiry.

But his original curiosity was not yet abated; he resolved to obtain some knowledge of the ways of men. His wish still continued, but his hope grew less. He ceased to survey any longer the walls of his prison, and spared to search by new toils for interstices which he knew could not be found, yet determined to keep his design always in view, and lay hold on any expedient that time should offer.

CHAPTER VI

A dissertation on the art of flying[19]

AMONG the artists[20] that had been allured into the happy valley, to labour for the accommodation and pleasure of its inhabitants, was a man eminent for his knowledge of the mechanick powers, who had contrived many engines both of use and recreation. By a wheel, which the stream turned, he forced the water into a tower, whence it was distributed to all the apartments of the palace. He erected a pavillion in the garden, around which he kept the air always cool by artificial showers. One of the groves, appropriated to the ladies, was ventilated by fans, to which the rivulet that run through it gave a constant motion; and instruments of soft musick were placed at proper distances, of which some played by the impulse of the wind, and some by the power of the stream.

This artist was sometimes visited by Rasselas, who was pleased with every kind of knowledge, imagining that the time would come when all his acquisitions should be of use to him in the open world. He came one day to amuse himself in his usual manner, and found the master busy in building a sailing chariot:[21] he saw that the design was practicable upon a level surface, and with expressions of great esteem solicited its completion. The workman was pleased to find himself so much regarded by the prince, and resolved to gain yet higher honours. 'Sir, said he, you have seen but a small part of what the mechanick sciences can perform. I have been long of opinion, that, instead of the tardy conveyance of ships and chariots, man might use the swifter migration of wings; that the fields of air are open to knowledge, and that only ignorance and idleness need crawl upon the ground.'

This hint rekindled the prince's desire of passing the mountains; having seen what the mechanist had already performed, he was willing to fancy that he could do more; yet resolved to inquire further before he suffered hope to afflict him by disappointment. 'I am afraid, said he to the artist, that your imagination prevails over your skill, and that you now tell me rather what you wish than what you know. Every animal has his element assigned him; the birds have the air, and man and beasts the earth.' 'So, replied the mechanist, fishes have the water, in which yet beasts can swim by nature, and men by art. He that can swim needs not despair to fly: to swim is to fly in a grosser fluid, and to fly is to swim in a subtler.[22] We are only to proportion our power of resistance to the different density of the matter through which we are to pass. You will be necessarily upborn by the air, if you can renew any impulse upon it, faster than the air can recede from the pressure.'

'But the exercise of swimming, said the prince, is very laborious; the strongest limbs are soon wearied; I am afraid the act of flying will be yet more violent, and wings will be of no great use, unless we can fly further than we can swim.'

'The labour of rising from the ground, said the artist, will be great, as we see it in the heavier domestick fowls; but, as we mount higher, the earth's attraction, and the body's gravity, will be gradually diminished, till we shall arrive at a region where the man will float in the air without any tendency to fall: no care will then be necessary, but to move forwards, which the gentlest impulse will effect. You, Sir, whose curiosity is so extensive, will easily conceive with what pleasure a philosopher, furnished with wings, and hovering in the sky, would see the earth, and all its inhabitants, rolling beneath him, and presenting to him successively, by its diurnal motion, all the countries within the same parallel. How must it amuse the pendent spectator to see the moving scene of land and ocean, cities and deserts! To survey with equal security the marts of trade, and the fields of battle; mountains infested by barbarians, and fruitful regions gladdened by plenty, and lulled by peace! How easily shall we then trace the Nile through all his passage; pass over to distant regions, and examine the face of nature from one extremity of the earth to the other!'

'All this, said the prince, is much to be desired, but I am afraid that no man will be able to breathe in these regions of speculation and tranquillity. I have been told, that respiration is difficult upon lofty mountains, yet from these precipices, though so high as to produce great tenuity of the air, it is very easy to fall: therefore I suspect, that from any height, where life can be supported, there may be danger of too quick descent.'

'Nothing, replied the artist, will ever be attempted, if all possible objections must be first overcome. If you will favour my project I will try the first flight at my own hazard. I have considered the structure of all volant animals, and find the folding continuity of the bat's wings most easily accommodated to the human form. Upon this model I shall begin my task to morrow, and in a year expect to tower into the air beyond the malice or pursuit of man. But I will work only on this condition, that the art shall not be divulged, and that you shall not require me to make wings for any but ourselves.'

'Why, said Rasselas, should you envy others so great an advantage? All skill ought to be exerted for universal good; every man has owed much to others, and ought to repay the kindness that he has received.'

'If men were all virtuous, returned the artist, I should with great alacrity teach them all to fly. But what would be the security of the good, if the bad could at pleasure invade them from the sky? Against an army sailing through the clouds neither walls, nor mountains, nor seas, could afford any security. A flight of northern savages might hover in the wind, and light at once with irresistible violence upon the capital of a fruitful region that was rolling under them. Even this valley, the retreat of princes, the abode of happiness, might be violated by the sudden descent of some of the naked nations that swarm on the coast of the southern sea.'

The prince promised secrecy, and waited for the performance, not wholly hopeless of success. He visited the work from time to time, observed its progress, and remarked many ingenious contrivances to facilitate motion, and unite levity[23] with strength. The artist was every day more certain that he should leave vultures and eagles behind him, and the contagion of his confidence seized upon the prince.

In a year the wings were finished, and, on a morning appointed, the maker appeared furnished for flight on a little promontory: he waved his pinions a while to gather air, then leaped from his stand, and in an instant dropped into the lake. His wings, which were of no use in the air, sustained him in the water, and the prince drew him to land, half dead with terrour and vexation.

CHAPTER VII

The prince finds a man of learning

THE prince was not much afflicted by this disaster, having suffered himself to hope for a happier event, only because he had no other means of escape in view. He still persisted in his design to leave the happy valley by the first opportunity.

His imagination was now at a stand; he had no prospect of entering into the world; and, notwithstanding all his endeavours to support himself,[24] discontent by degrees preyed upon him, and he began to lose his thoughts in sadness, when the rainy season, which in these countries is periodical, made it inconvenient to wander in the woods.

The rain continued longer and with more violence than had been ever known: the clouds broke on the surrounding mountains, and the torrents streamed into the plain on every side, till the cavern was too narrow to discharge the water. The lake overflowed its banks, and all the level of the valley was covered with the inundation. The eminence, on which the palace was built, and some other spots of rising ground, were all that the eye could now discover. The herds and flocks left the pastures, and both the wild beasts and the tame retreated to the mountains.

This inundation confined all the princes to domestick amusements, and the attention of Rasselas was particularly seized by a poem, which Imlac[25] rehearsed,[26] upon the various conditions of humanity. He commanded the poet to attend him in his apartment, and recite his verses a second time; then entering into familiar talk, he thought himself happy in having found a man who knew the world so well, and could so skilfully paint the scenes of life. He asked a thousand questions about things, to which, though common to all other mortals, his confinement from childhood had kept him a stranger. The poet pitied his ignorance, and loved his curiosity,[27] and entertained him from day to day with novelty and instruction, so that the prince regretted the necessity of sleep, and longed till the morning should renew his pleasure.

As they were sitting together, the prince commanded Imlac to relate his history, and to tell by what accident he was forced, or by what motive induced, to close his life in the happy valley. As he was going to begin his narrative, Rasselas was called to a concert, and obliged to restrain his curiosity till the evening.

CHAPTER VIII

The history of Imlac

THE close of the day is, in the regions of the torrid zone, the only season of diversion and entertainment, and it was therefore mid-night before the musick ceased, and the princesses retired. Rasselas then called for his companion and required him to begin the story of his life.

'Sir, said Imlac, my history will not be long: the life that is devoted to knowledge passes silently away, and is very little diversified by events. To talk in publick, to think in solitude, to read and to hear, to inquire, and answer inquiries, is the business of a scholar. He wanders about the world without pomp or terrour, and is neither known nor valued but by men like himself.

'I was born in the kingdom of Goiama,[28] at no great distance from the fountain of the Nile.[29] My father was a wealthy merchant, who traded between the inland countries of Africk and the ports of the Red Sea. He was honest, frugal and diligent, but of mean[30] sentiments, and narrow comprehension: he desired only to be rich, and to conceal his riches, lest he should be spoiled[31] by the governors of the province.'

'Surely, said the prince, my father must be negligent of his charge, if any man in his dominions dares take that which belongs to another. Does he not know that kings are accountable for injustice permitted as well as done? If I were emperour, not the meanest of my subjects should be oppressed with impunity. My blood boils when I am told that a merchant durst not enjoy his honest gains for fear of losing them by the rapacity of power. Name the governor who robbed the people, that I may declare his crimes to the emperour.'

'Sir, said Imlac, your ardour is the natural effect of virtue animated by youth: the time will come when you will acquit your father, and perhaps hear with less impatience of the governor. Oppression is, in the Abissinian dominions, neither frequent nor tolerated; but no form of government has been yet discovered, by which cruelty can be wholly prevented. Subordination supposes power on one part and subjection on the other; and if power be in the hands of men, it will sometimes be abused. The vigilance of the supreme magistrate[32] may do much, but much will still remain undone. He can never know all the crimes that are committed, and can seldom punish all that he knows.'

'This, said the prince, I do not understand, but I had rather hear thee than dispute. Continue thy narration.'

'My father, proceeded Imlac, originally intended that I should have no other education, than such as might qualify me for commerce; and discovering in me great strength of memory, and quickness of apprehension, often declared his hope that I should be some time the richest man in Abissinia.'

'Why, said the prince, did thy father desire the increase of his wealth, when it was already greater than he durst discover[33] or enjoy? I am unwilling to doubt thy veracity, yet inconsistencies cannot both be true.'

'Inconsistencies, answered Imlac, cannot both be right, but, imputed to man, they may both be true. Yet diversity is not inconsistency. My father might expect a time of greater security. However, some desire is necessary to keep life in motion, and he, whose real wants are supplied, must admit those of fancy.'

'This, said the prince, I can in some measure conceive. I repent that I interrupted thee.'

'With this hope, proceeded Imlac, he sent me to school; but when I had once found the delight of knowledge, and felt the pleasure of intelligence and the pride of invention,[34] I began silently to despise riches, and determined to disappoint the purpose of my father, whose grossness of conception raised my pity. I was twenty years old before his tenderness would expose me to the fatigue of travel, in which time I had been instructed, by successive masters, in all the literature of my native country. As every hour taught me something new, I lived in a continual course of gratifications; but, as I advanced towards manhood, I lost much of the reverence with which I had been used to look on my instructors; because, when the lesson was ended, I did not find them wiser or better than common men.

'At length my father resolved to initiate me in commerce, and, opening one of his subterranean treasuries, counted out ten thousand pieces of gold. This, young man, said he, is the stock with which you must negotiate.[35] I began with less than the fifth part, and you see how diligence and parsimony[36] have increased it. This is your own to waste or to improve. If you squander it by negligence or caprice, you must wait for my death before you will be rich: if, in four years, you double your stock, we will thenceforward let subordination cease, and live together as friends and partners; for he shall always be equal with me, who is equally skilled in the art of growing rich.

'We laid our money upon camels, concealed in bales of cheap goods, and travelled to the shore of the Red Sea. When I cast my eye on the expanse of waters my heart bounded like that of a prisoner escaped. I felt an unextinguishable curiosity kindle in my mind, and resolved to snatch this opportunity of seeing the manners of other nations, and of learning sciences[37] unknown in Abissinia.

'I remembered that my father had obliged[38] me to the improvement of my stock, not by a promise which I ought not to violate, but by a penalty which I was at liberty to incur; and therefore determined to gratify my predominant desire, and by drinking at the fountains of knowledge, to quench the thirst of curiosity.

'As I was supposed to trade without connexion with my father, it was easy for me to become acquainted with the master of a ship, and procure a passage to some other country. I had no motives of choice to regulate my voyage; it was sufficient for me that, wherever I wandered, I should see a country which I had not seen before. I therefore entered a ship bound for Surat,[39] having left a letter for my father declaring my intention.

CHAPTER IX

The history of Imlac continued

WHEN I first entered upon the world of waters, and lost sight of land, I looked round about me with pleasing terrour, and thinking my soul enlarged by the boundless prospect, imagined that I could gaze round for ever without satiety; but, in a short time, I grew weary of looking on barren uniformity, where I could only see again what I had already seen. I then descended into the ship, and doubted for a while whether all my future pleasures would not end like this in disgust and disappointment. Yet, surely, said I, the ocean and the land are very different; the only variety of water is rest and motion, but the earth has mountains and vallies, deserts and cities: it is inhabited by men of different customs and contrary opinions; and I may hope to find variety in life, though I should miss it in nature.

'With this thought I quieted my mind; and amused myself during the voyage, sometimes by learning from the sailors the art of navigation, which I have never practised, and sometimes by forming schemes for my conduct in different situations, in not one of which I have been ever placed.

'I was almost weary of my naval amusements when we landed safely at Surat. I secured my money, and purchasing some commodities for show,[40] joined myself to a caravan that was passing into the inland country. My companions, for some reason or other, conjecturing that I was rich, and, by my inquiries and admiration,[41] finding that I was ignorant, considered me as a novice whom they had a right to cheat, and who was to learn at the usual expence the art of fraud. They exposed me to the theft of servants, and the exaction of officers, and saw me plundered upon false pretences, without any advantage to themselves, but that of rejoicing in the superiority of their own knowledge.'

'Stop a moment, said the prince. Is there such depravity in man, as that he should injure another without benefit to himself? I can easily conceive that all are pleased with superiority; but your ignorance was merely accidental, which, being neither your crime nor your folly, could afford them no reason to applaud themselves; and the knowledge which they had, and which you wanted, they might as effectively have shown by warning, as betraying you.'

'Pride, said Imlac, is seldom delicate, it will please itself with very mean advantages; and envy feels not its own happiness, but when it may be compared with the misery of others. They were my enemies because they grieved to think me rich, and my oppressors beçause they delighted to find me weak.'

'Proceed, said the prince: I doubt not of the facts which you relate, but imagine that you impute them to mistaken motives.'

'In this company, said Imlac, I arrived at Agra, the capital of Indostan,[42] the city in which the great Mogul[43] commonly resides. I applied myself to the language of the country, and in a few months was able to converse with the learned men; some of whom I found morose and reserved, and others easy and communicative; some were unwilling to teach another what they had with difficulty learned themselves; and some showed that the end of their studies was to gain the dignity of instructing.

'To the tutor of the young princes I recommended myself so much, that I was presented to the emperour as a man of uncommon knowledge. The emperour asked me many questions concerning my country and my travels; and though I cannot now recollect anything that he uttered above the power of a common man, he dismissed me astonished at his wisdom, and enamoured of his goodness.

'My credit was now so high, that the merchants, with whom I had travelled, applied to me for recommendations to the ladies of the court. I was surprised at their confidence of solicitation, and gently reproached them with their practices on the road. They heard me with cold indifference, and showed no tokens of shame or sorrow.

'They then urged their request with the offer of a bribe; but what I would not do for kindness I would not do for money; and refused them, not because they had injured me, but because I would not enable them to injure others; for I knew they would have made use of my credit to cheat those who should buy their wares.

'Having resided at Agra till there was no more to be learned, I travelled into Persia, where I saw many remains of ancient magnificence, and observed many new accommodations[44] of life. The Persians are a nation eminently social, and their assemblies afforded me daily opportunities of remarking characters and manners, and of tracing human nature through all its variations.

'From Persia I passed into Arabia, where I saw a nation at once pastoral and warlike; who live without any settled habitation; whose only wealth is their flocks and herds; and who have yet carried on, through all ages, an hereditary war with all mankind, though they neither covet nor envy their possessions.

CHAPTER X

Imlac's history continued. A dissertation upon poetry

WHEREVER I went, I found that Poetry was considered as the highest learning, and regarded with a veneration somewhat approaching to that which man would pay to the Angelick Nature. And it yet fills me with wonder, that, in almost all countries, the most ancient poets are considered as the best: whether it be that every other kind of knowledge is an acquisition gradually attained, and poetry is a gift conferred at once; or that the first poetry of every nation surprised them as a novelty, and retained the credit by consent which it received by accident at first: or whether, as the province of poetry is to describe Nature and Passion, which are always the same, the first writers took possession of the most striking objects for description, and the most probable occurrences for fiction, and left nothing to those that followed them, but transcription of the same events, and new combinations of the same images. Whatever be the reason, it is commonly observed that the early writers are in possession of nature, and their followers of art: that the first excel in strength and invention, and the latter in elegance and refinement.

'I was desirous to add my name to this illustrious fraternity. I read all the poets of Persia and Arabia, and was able to repeat by memory the volumes that are suspended [45] in the mosque of Mecca. But I soon found that no man was ever great by imitation. My desire of excellence impelled me to transfer my attention to nature and to life. Nature was to be my subject, and men to be my auditors: I could never describe what I had not seen: I could not hope to move those with delight or terrour, whose interests and opinions I did not understand.

'Being now resolved to be a poet, I saw every thing with a new purpose; my sphere of attention was suddenly magnified: no kind of knowledge was to be overlooked. I ranged mountains and deserts for images and resemblances, and pictured upon my mind every tree of the forest and flower of the valley. I observed with equal care the crags of the rock and the pinnacles of the palace. Sometimes I wandered along the mazes of the rivulet, and sometimes watched the changes of the summer clouds. To a poet nothing can be useless. Whatever is beautiful, and whatever is dreadful,[46] must be familiar to his imagination: he must be conversant with all that is awfully vast or elegantly little. The plants of the garden, the animals of the wood, the minerals of the earth, and meteors of the sky, must all concur to store his mind with inexhaustible variety: for every idea is useful for the enforcement or decoration of moral or religious truth; and he, who knows most, will have most power of diversifying his scenes, and of gratifying his reader with remote allusions and unexpected instruction.

'All the appearances of nature I was therefore careful to study, and every country which I have surveyed has contributed something to my poetical powers.'

'In so wide a survey, said the prince, you must surely have left much unobserved. I have lived, till now, within the circuit of these mountains, and yet cannot walk abroad without the sight of something which I had never beheld before, or never heeded.'

'The business of a poet, said Imlac, is to examine, not the individual, but the species; to remark general properties and large appearances: he does not number the streaks of the tulip, or describe the different shades in the verdure of the forest. He is to exhibit in his portraits of nature such prominent and striking features, as recall the original to every mind; and must neglect the minuter discriminations, which one may have remarked, and another have neglected, for those characteristicks which are alike obvious to vigilance and carelessness.

'But the knowledge of nature is only half the task of a poet; he must be acquainted likewise with all the modes of life. His character [47] requires that he estimate the happiness and misery of every condition; observe the power of all the passions in all their combinations, and trace the changes of the human mind as they are modified by various institutions and accidental influences of climate or custom, from the spriteliness of infancy to the despondence of decrepitude. He must divest himself of the prejudices of his age or country; he must consider right and wrong in their abstracted and invariable state; he must disregard present laws and opinions, and rise to general and transcendental [48] truths, which will always be the same: he must therefore content himself with the slow progress of his name; contemn [49] the applause of his own time, and commit his claims to the justice of posterity. He must write as the interpreter of nature, and the legislator of mankind, [50] and consider himself as presiding over the thoughts and manners of future generations; as a being superiour to time and place.

'His labour is not yet at an end: he must know many languages and many sciences; and, that his stile may be worthy of his thoughts, must, by incessant practice, familiarize to himself every delicacy of speech and grace of harmony.'

CHAPTER XI

Imlac's narrative continued. A hint on pilgrimage

IMLAC now felt the enthusiastic[51] fit, and was proceeding to aggrandize his own profession, when the prince cried out, 'Enough! Thou hast convinced me, that no human being can ever be a poet. Proceed with thy narration.'

'To be a poet, said Imlac, is indeed very difficult.' 'So difficult, returned the prince, that I will at present hear no more of his labours. Tell me whither you went when you had seen Persia.'

'From Persia, said the poet, I travelled through Syria, and for three years resided in Palestine, where I conversed with great numbers of the northern and western nations of Europe; the nations which are now in possession of all power and all knowledge; whose armies are irresistible, and whose fleets command the remotest parts of the globe. When I compared these men with the natives of our own kingdom, and those that surround us, they appeared almost another order of beings. In their countries it is difficult to wish for any thing that may not be obtained: a thousand arts, of which we never heard, are continually labouring for their convenience and pleasure; and whatever their own climate has denied them is supplied by their commerce.'

'By what means, said the prince, are the Europeans thus powerful? or why, since they can so easily visit Asia and Africa for trade or conquest, cannot the Asiaticks and Africans invade their coasts, plant colonies in their ports, and give laws to their natural[52] princes? The same wind that carries them back would bring us thither.'

'They are more powerful, Sir, than we, answered Imlac, because they are wiser; knowledge will always predominate over ignorance, as man governs the other animals. But why their knowledge is more than ours, I know not what reason can be given, but the unsearchable will of the Supreme Being.'

'When, said the prince with a sigh, shall I be able to visit Palestine, and mingle with this mighty confluence of nations? Till that happy moment shall arrive, let me fill up the time with such representations as thou canst give me. I am not ignorant of the motive that assembles such numbers in that place, and cannot but consider it as the center of wisdom and piety, to which the best and wisest men of every land must be continually resorting.'

'There are some nations, said Imlac, that send few visitants to Palestine; for many numerous and learned sects in Europe, concur to censure pilgrimage as superstitious, or deride it as ridiculous.'

'You know, said the prince, how little my life has made me acquainted with diversity of opinions: it will be too long to hear the arguments on both sides; you, that have considered them, tell me the result.'

'Pilgrimage, said Imlac, like many other acts of piety, may be reasonable or superstitious, according to the principles upon which it is performed. Long journeys in search of truth are not commanded. Truth, such as is necessary to the regulation of life, is always found where it is honestly sought. Change of place is no natural cause of the increase of piety, for it inevitably produces dissipation of mind. Yet, since men go every day to view the fields where great actions have been performed, and return with stronger impressions of the event, curiosity of the same kind may naturally dispose us to view that country whence our religion[53] had its beginning; and I believe no man surveys those awful scenes without some confirmation of holy resolutions. That the Supreme Being may be more easily propitiated in one place than in another, is the dream of idle superstition; but that some places may operate upon our own minds in an uncommon manner, is an opinion which hourly experience will justify. He who supposes that his vices may be more successfully combated in Palestine, will, perhaps, find himself mistaken, yet he may go thither without folly: he who thinks they will be more freely pardoned, dishonours at once his reason and religion.'

'These, said the prince, are European distinctions. I will consider them another time. What have you found to be the effect of knowledge? Are those nations happier than we?'

'There is so much infelicity, said the poet, in the world, that scarce any man has leisure from his own distresses to estimate the comparative happiness of others. Knowledge is certainly one of the means of pleasure, as is confessed by the natural desire which every mind feels of increasing its ideas. Ignorance is mere privation, by which nothing can be produced: it is a vacuity in which the soul sits motionless and torpid for want of attraction; and, without knowing why, we always rejoice when we learn, and grieve when we forget. I am therefore inclined to conclude, that, if nothing counteracts the natural consequence of learning, we grow more happy as our minds take a wider range.

'In enumerating the particular comforts of life we shall find many advantages on the side of the Europeans. They cure wounds and diseases with which we languish and perish. We suffer inclemencies of weather which they can obviate. They have engines for the despatch of many laborious works, which we must perform by manual industry. There is such communication between distant places, that one friend can hardly be said to be absent from another. Their policy[54] removes all publick inconveniencies: they have roads cut through their mountains, and bridges laid upon their rivers. And, if we descend to the privacies of life, their habitations are more commodious, and their possessions are more secure.'

'They are surely happy, said the prince, who have all these conveniencies, of which I envy none so much as the facility with which separated friends interchange their thoughts.'

'The Europeans, answered Imlac, are less unhappy than we, but they are not happy. Human life is every where a state in which much is to be endured, and little to be enjoyed.'

CHAPTER XII

The story of Imlac continued

'I AM not yet willing, said the prince, to suppose that happiness is so parsimoniously distributed to mortals; nor can believe but that, if I had the choice of life, I should be able to fill every day with pleasure. I would injure no man, and should provoke no resentment: I would relieve every distress, and should enjoy the benedictions of gratitude. I would choose my friends among the wise, and my wife among the virtuous; and therefore should be in no danger from treachery, or unkindness. My children should, by my care, be learned and pious, and would repay to my age what their childhood had received. What would dare to molest him who might call on every side to thousands enriched by his bounty, or assisted by his power? And why should not life glide quietly away in the soft reciprocation of protection and reverence? All this may be done without the help of European refinements, which appear by their effects to be rather specious than useful. Let us leave them and pursue our journey.'

'From Palestine, said Imlac, I passed through many regions of Asia; in the more civilized kingdoms as a trader, and among the Barbarians of the mountains as a pilgrim. At last I began to long for my native country, that I might repose after my travels, and fatigues, in the places where I had spent my earliest years, and gladden my old companions with the recital of my adventures. Often did I figure to myself those, with whom I had sported away the gay hours of dawning life, sitting round me in its evening, wondering at my tales, and listening to my counsels.

'When this thought had taken possession of my mind, I considered every moment as wasted which did not bring me nearer to Abissinia. I hastened into Egypt, and, notwithstanding my impatience, was detained ten months in the contemplation of its ancient magnificence, and in inquiries after the remains of its ancient learning. I found in Cairo a mixture of all nations; some brought thither by the love of knowledge, some by the hope of gain, and many by the desire of living after their own manner without observation, and of lying hid in the obscurity of multitudes: for, in a city, populous as Cairo, it is possible to obtain at the same time the gratifications of society, and the secrecy of solitude.

'From Cairo I travelled to Suez, and embarked on the Red Sea, passing along the coast till I arrived at the port from which I had departed twenty years before. Here I joined myself to a caravan and re-entered my native country.

'I now expected the caresses of my kinsmen, and the congratulations of my friends, and was not without hope that my father, whatever value he had set upon riches, would own with gladness and pride a son who was able to add to the felicity and honour of the nation. But I was soon convinced that my thoughts were vain. My father had been dead fourteen years, having divided his wealth among my brothers, who were removed to some other provinces. Of my companions the greater part was in the grave, of the rest some could with difficulty remember me, and some considered me as one corrupted by foreign manners.

'A man used to vicissitudes is not easily dejected. I forgot, after a time, my disappointment, and endeavoured to recommend myself to the nobles of the kingdom: they admitted me to their tables, heard my story, and dismissed me. I opened a school, and was prohibited to teach. I then resolved to sit down in the quiet of domestick life, and addressed[55] a lady that was fond of my conversation, but rejected my suit, because my father was a merchant.

'Wearied at last with solicitation and repulses, I resolved to hide myself for ever from the world, and depend no longer on the opinion or caprice of others. I waited for the time when the gate of the *happy valley* should open, that I might bid farewell to hope and fear: the day came; my performance was distinguished with favour, and I resigned myself with joy to perpetual confinement.'

'Hast thou here found happiness at last? said Rasselas. Tell me without reserve; art thou content with thy condition? or, dost thou wish to be again wandering and inquiring? All the inhabitants of this valley celebrate their lot, and, at the annual visit of the emperour, invite others to partake of their felicity.'

'Great prince, said Imlac, I shall speak the truth: I know not one of all your attendants who does not lament the hour when he entered this retreat. I am less unhappy than the rest, because I have a mind replete with images, which I can vary and combine at pleasure. I can amuse my solitude by the renovation of the knowledge which begins to fade from my memory, and by recollection of the accidents of my past life. Yet all this ends in the sorrowful consideration, that my acquirements are now useless, and that none of my pleasures can be again enjoyed. The rest, whose minds have no impression but of the present moment, are either corroded by malignant passions, or sit stupid in the gloom of perpetual vacancy.'

'What passions can infest those, said the prince, who have no rivals? We are in a place where impotence precludes malice, and where all envy is repressed by community of enjoyments.'

'There may be community, said Imlac, of material possessions, but there can never be community of love or of esteem. It must happen that one will please more than another; he that knows himself despised will always be envious; and still more envious and malevolent, if he is condemned to live in the presence of those who despise him. The invitations, by which they allure others to a state which they feel to be wretched, proceed from the natural malignity of hopeless misery. They are weary of themselves, and of each other, and expect to find relief in new companions. They envy the liberty which their folly has forfeited, and would gladly see all mankind imprisoned like themselves.

'From this crime, however, I am wholly free. No man can say that he is wretched by my persuasion. I look with pity on the crowds who are annually soliciting admission to captivity, and wish that it were lawful for me to warn them of their danger.'

'My dear Imlac, said the prince, I will open to thee my whole heart. I have long meditated an escape from the happy valley. I have examined the mountains on every side, but find myself insuperably barred: teach me the way to break my prison; thou shalt be the companion of my flight, the guide of my rambles, the partner of my fortune, and my sole director in the *choice of life*.'

'Sir, answered the poet, your escape will be difficult, and, perhaps, you may soon repent your curiosity. The world, which you figure to yourself smooth and quiet as the lake in the valley, you will find a sea foaming with tempests, and boiling with whirlpools: you will be sometimes overwhelmed by the waves of violence, and sometimes dashed against the rocks of treachery. Amidst wrongs and frauds, competitions and anxieties, you will wish a thousand times for these seats of quiet, and willingly quit hope to be free from fear.'

'Do not seek to deter me from my purpose, said the prince: I am impatient to see what thou hast seen; and, since thou art thyself weary of the valley, it is evident, that thy former state was better than this. Whatever be the consequence of my experiment, I am resolved to judge with my own eyes of the various conditions of men, and then to make deliberately my *choice of life*.'

'I am afraid, said Imlac, you are hindered by stronger restraints than my persuasions; yet, if your determination is fixed, I do not counsel you to despair. Few things are impossible to diligence and skill.'

CHAPTER XIII

Rasselas discovers the means of escape

THE prince now dismissed his favourite to rest, but the narrative of wonders and novelties filled his mind with perturbation.[56] He revolved all that he had heard, and prepared innumerable questions for the morning.

Much of his uneasiness was now removed. He had a friend to whom he could impart his thoughts, and whose experience could assist him in his designs. His heart was no longer condemned to swell with silent vexation. He thought that even the *happy valley* might be endured with such a companion, and that, if they could range the world together, he should have nothing further to desire.

In a few days the water was discharged, and the ground dried. The prince and Imlac then walked out together to converse without the notice of the rest. The prince, whose thoughts were always on the wing, as he passed by the gate, said, with a countenance of sorrow, 'Why art thou so strong, and why is man so weak?'

'Man is not weak, answered his companion; knowledge is more than equivalent to force. The master of mechanicks laughs at strength. I can burst the gate, but cannot do it secretly. Some other expedient must be tried.'

As they were walking on the side of the mountain, they observed that the conies, which the rain had driven from their burrows, had taken shelter among the bushes, and formed holes behind them, tending upwards in an oblique line. 'It has been the opinion of antiquity, said Imlac, that human reason borrowed many arts from the instinct of animals; let us, therefore, not think ourselves degraded by learning from the coney. We may escape by piercing the mountain in the same direction. We will begin where the summit hangs over the middle part, and labour upward till we shall issue out beyond the prominence.'

The eyes of the prince, when he heard this proposal, sparkled with joy. The execution was easy, and the success certain.

No time was now lost. They hastened early in the morning to choose a place proper for their mine. They clambered with great fatigue among crags and brambles, and returned without having discovered any part that favoured their design. The second and the third day were spent in the same manner, and with the same frustration. But, on the fourth, they found a small cavern, concealed by a thicket, where they resolved to make their experiment.

Imlac procured instruments proper to hew stone and remove earth, and they fell to their work on the next day with more eagerness than vigour. They were presently exhausted by their efforts, and sat down to pant upon the grass. The prince, for a moment, appeared to be discouraged. 'Sir, said his companion, practice will enable us to continue our labour for a longer time; mark, however, how far we have advanced, and you will find that our toil will some time have an end. Great works are performed, not by strength, but perseverance: yonder palace was raised by single stones, yet you see its height and spaciousness. He that shall walk with vigour three hours a day will pass in seven years a space equal to the circumference of the globe.'

They returned to their work day after day, and, in a short time, found a fissure in the rock, which enabled them to pass far with very little obstruction. This Rasselas considered as a good omen. 'Do not disturb your mind, said Imlac, with other hopes or fears than reason may suggest: if you are pleased with prognosticks of good, you will be terrified likewise with tokens of evil, and your whole life will be a prey to superstition. Whatever facilitates our work is more than an omen, it is a cause of success. This is one of those pleasing surprises which often happen to active resolution. Many things difficult to design prove easy to performance.'

CHAPTER XIV

Rasselas and Imlac receive an unexpected visit

THEY had now wrought their way to the middle, and solaced their toil with the approach of liberty, when the prince, coming down to refresh himself with air, found his sister Nekayah standing before the mouth of the cavity. He started and stood confused, afraid to tell his design, and yet hopeless to conceal it. A few moments determined him to repose on[57] her fidelity, and secure her secrecy by a declaration without reserve.

'Do not imagine, said the princess, that I came hither as a spy: I had long observed from my window, that you and Imlac directed your walk every day towards the same point, but I did not suppose you had any better reason for the preference than a cooler shade, or more fragrant bank; nor followed you with any other design than to partake of your conversation. Since then not suspicion but fondness has detected you, let me not lose the advantage of my discovery. I am equally weary of confinement with yourself,[58] and not less desirous of knowing what is done or suffered in the world. Permit me to fly with you from this tasteless tranquillity, which will yet grow more loathsome when you have left me. You may deny me to accompany you, but cannot hinder me from following.'

The prince, who loved Nekayah above his other sisters, had no inclination to refuse her request, and grieved that he had lost an opportunity of showing his confidence by a voluntary communication. It was therefore agreed that she should leave the valley with them; and that, in the mean time, she should watch, lest any other straggler should, by chance or curiosity, follow them to the mountain.

At length their labour was at an end; they saw light beyond the prominence, and, issuing to the top of the mountain, beheld the Nile, yet a narrow current, wandering beneath them.

The prince looked round with rapture, anticipated all the pleasures of travel, and in thought was already transported beyond his father's dominions. Imlac, though very joyful at his escape, had less expectation of pleasure in the world, which he had before tried, and of which he had been weary.

Rasselas was so much delighted with a wider horizon, that he could not soon be persuaded to return into the valley. He informed his sister that the way was open, and that nothing now remained but to prepare for their departure.

CHAPTER XV

The prince and princess leave the valley, and see many wonders

THE prince and princess had jewels sufficient to make them rich whenever they came into a place of commerce, which, by Imlac's direction, they hid in their cloaths, and, on the night of the next full moon, all left the valley. The princess was followed only by a single favourite, who did not know whither she was going.

They clambered through the cavity, and began to go down on the other side. The princess and her maid turned their eyes towards every part, and, seeing nothing to bound their prospect, considered themselves as in danger of being lost in a dreary[59] vacuity. They stopped and trembled. 'I am almost afraid, said the princess, to begin a journey of which I cannot perceive an end, and to venture into this immense plain where I may be approached on every side by men whom I never saw.' The prince felt nearly the same emotions, though he thought it more manly to conceal them.

Imlac smiled at their terrours, and encouraged them to

proceed; but the princess continued irresolute till she had been imperceptibly drawn forward too far to return.

In the morning they found some shepherds in the field, who set milk and fruits before them. The princess wondered that she did not see a palace ready for her reception, and a table spread with delicacies; but, being faint and hungry, she drank the milk and eat the fruits, and thought them of a higher flavour than the products of the valley.

They travelled forward by easy journeys, being all unaccustomed to toil or difficulty, and knowing, that though they might be missed, they could not be pursued. In a few days they came into a more populous region, where Imlac was diverted with the admiration which his companions expressed at the diversity of manners, stations[60] and employments.

Their dress was such as might not bring upon them the suspicion of having any thing to conceal, yet the prince, wherever he came, expected to be obeyed, and the princess was frighted, because those that came into her presence did not prostrate themselves before her. Imlac was forced to observe them with great vigilance, lest they should betray their rank by their unusual behaviour, and detained them several weeks in the first village to accustom them to the sight of common mortals.

By degrees the royal wanderers were taught to understand that they had for a time laid aside their dignity, and were to expect only such regard as liberality and courtesy could procure. And Imlac, having, by many admonitions, prepared them to endure the tumults of a port, and the ruggedness[61] of the commercial race, brought them down to the sea-coast.

The prince and his sister, to whom every thing was new, were gratified equally at all places, and therefore remained for some months at the port without any inclination to pass further. Imlac was content with their stay, because he did not think it safe to expose them, unpractised in the world, to the hazards of a foreign country.

At last he began to fear lest they should be discovered,

and proposed to fix a day for their departure. They had no pretensions to judge for themselves, and referred the whole scheme to his direction. He therefore took passage in a ship to Suez; and, when the time came, with great difficulty prevailed on the princess to enter the vessel. They had a quick and prosperous voyage, and from Suez travelled by land to Cairo.

CHAPTER XVI

They enter Cairo, and find every man happy

As they approached the city, which filled the strangers with astonishment, 'This, said Imlac to the prince, is the place where travellers and merchants assemble from all the corners of the earth. You will here find men of every character, and every occupation. Commerce is here honourable: I will act as a merchant, and you shall live as strangers, who have no other end of travel than curiosity; it will soon be observed that we are rich; our reputation will procure us access to all whom we shall desire to know; you will see all the conditions of humanity, and enable yourself at leisure to make your *choice of life*.'

They now entered the town, stunned by the noise, and offended by the crowds. Instruction had not yet so prevailed over habit, but that they wondered to see themselves pass undistinguished along the street, and met by the lowest of the people without reverence or notice. The princess could not at first bear the thought of being levelled with the vulgar,[62] and, for some days, continued in her chamber, where she was served by her favourite Pekuah as in the palace of the valley.

Imlac, who understood traffick,[63] sold part of the jewels the next day, and hired a house, which he adorned with such magnificence, that he was immediately considered as a merchant of great wealth. His politeness attracted many acquaintance, and his generosity made him courted by many dependants. His table was crowded by men of every nation, who all admired his knowledge, and solicited his favour. His companions, not being able to mix in the conversation, could make no discovery of[64] their ignorance or surprise, and were gradually initiated in the world as they gained knowledge of the language.

The prince had, by frequent lectures, been taught the use and nature of money; but the ladies could not, for a long time, comprehend what the merchants did with small pieces of gold and silver, or why things of so little use should be received as equivalent to the necessaries of life.

They studied the language two years, while Imlac was preparing to set before them the various ranks and conditions of mankind. He grew acquainted with all who had any thing uncommon in their fortune or conduct. He frequented the voluptuous[65] and the frugal, the idle and the busy, the merchants and the men of learning.

The prince, being now able to converse with fluency, and having learned the caution necessary to be observed in his intercourse with strangers, began to accompany Imlac to places of resort, and to enter into all assemblies, that he might make his *choice of life*.

For some time he thought choice needless, because all appeared to him equally happy. Wherever he went he met gaiety and kindness, and heard the song of joy, or the laugh of carelessness. He began to believe that the world overflowed with universal plenty, and that nothing was withheld either from want or merit; that every hand showered liberality, and every heart melted with benevolence: 'and who then, says he, will be suffered to be wretched?'

Imlac permitted the pleasing delusion, and was unwilling to crush the hope of inexperience; till one day, having sat a while silent, 'I know not, said the prince, what can be the reason that I am more unhappy than any of our friends. I see them perpetually and unalterably cheerful, but feel my own mind restless and uneasy. I am unsatisfied with those pleasures which I seem most to court; I live in the crowds of jollity, not so much to enjoy company as to shun myself,[66] and am only loud and merry to conceal my sadness.'

'Every man, said Imlac, may, by examining his own mind, guess what passes in the minds of others: when you feel that your own gaiety is counterfeit, it may justly lead you to suspect that of your companions not to be sincere. Envy is commonly reciprocal. We are long before we are convinced that happiness is never to be found, and each believes it possessed by others, to keep alive the hope of obtaining it for himself. In the assembly, where you passed the last night, there appeared such spriteliness of air, and volatility of fancy, as might have suited beings of an higher order, formed to inhabit serener regions inaccessible to care or sorrow: yet, believe me, prince, there was not one who did not dread the moment when solitude should deliver him to the tyranny of reflection.'

'This, said the prince, may be true of others, since it is true of me; yet, whatever be the general infelicity of man, one condition is more happy than another, and wisdom surely directs us to take the least evil in the *choice of life*.'

'The causes of good and evil, answered Imlac, are so various and uncertain, so often entangled with each other, so diversified by various relations, and so much subject to accidents which cannot be foreseen, that he who would fix his condition upon incontestable reasons of preference, must live and die inquiring and deliberating.'

'But surely, said Rasselas, the wise men, to whom we listen with reverence and wonder, chose that mode of life for themselves which they thought most likely to make them happy.'

'Very few, said the poet, live by choice. Every man is placed in his present condition by causes which acted without his foresight, and with which he did not always willingly co-operate; and therefore you will rarely meet one who does not think the lot of his neighbour better than his own.'

'I am pleased to think, said the prince, that my birth has given me at least one advantage over others, by enabling me to determine for myself. I have here the world before me; I will review it at leisure: surely happiness is somewhere to be found.'

CHAPTER XVII

The prince associates with young men of spirit and gaiety

RASSELAS rose next day, and resolved to begin his experiments upon life. 'Youth, cried he, is the time of gladness: I will join myself to the young men, whose only business is to gratify their desires, and whose time is all spent in a succession of enjoyments.'

To such societies he was readily admitted, but a few days brought him back weary and disgusted. Their mirth was without images,[67] their laughter without motive; their pleasures were gross and sensual in which the mind had no part; their conduct was at once wild and mean; they laughed at order and at law, but the frown of power dejected, and the eye of wisdom abashed them.

The prince soon concluded, that he should never be happy in a course of life of which he was ashamed. He thought it unsuitable to a reasonable being to act without a plan, and to be sad or cheerful only by chance. 'Happiness, said he, must be something solid and permanent, without fear and without uncertainty.'

But his young companions had gained so much of his regard by their frankness and courtesy, that he could not leave them without warning and remonstrance. 'My friends, said he, I have seriously considered our manners and our prospects, and find that we have mistaken our own interest. The first years of man must make provision for the last. He that never thinks never can be wise. Perpetual levity must end in ignorance; and intemperance, though it may fire the spirits for an hour, will make life short or miserable. Let us consider that youth is of no long duration, and that in maturer age, when the enchantments of fancy shall cease, and phantoms of delight dance no more about us, we shall have no comforts but the esteem of wise men, and the means of doing good. Let us, therefore, stop, while to stop is in our power: let us live as men who are sometime to grow old, and to whom it will be the most dreadful of all evils not to count their past years but by follies, and to be reminded of their former luxuriance of health only by the maladies which riot has produced.'

They stared a while in silence one upon another, and, at last, drove him away by a general chorus of continued laughter.

The consciousness that his sentiments were just, and his intentions kind, was scarcely sufficient to support him against the horrour of derision. But he recovered his tranquillity, and pursued his search.

CHAPTER XVIII

The prince finds a wise and happy man

As he was one day walking in the street, he saw a spacious building which all were, by the open doors, invited to enter: he followed the stream of people, and found it a hall or school of declamation, in which professors read lectures to their auditory.[68] He fixed his eye upon a sage raised above the rest, who discoursed with great energy on the government of the passions. His look was venerable, his action graceful, his pronunciation clear, and his diction elegant. He showed, with great strength of sentiment, and variety of illustration, that human nature is degraded and debased, when the lower faculties predominate over the higher; that when fancy, the parent of passion, usurps the domination of the mind, nothing ensues but the natural effect of unlawful government, perturbation and confusion; that she betrays the fortresses of the intellect to rebels, and excites her children to sedition against reason their lawful sovereign. He compared reason to the sun, of which the light is constant, uniform, and lasting; and fancy to a meteor, of bright but transitory lustre, irregular in its motion, and delusive in its direction.

He then communicated the various precepts given from time to time for the conquest of passion, and displayed the happiness of those who had obtained the important victory, after which man is no longer the slave of fear, nor the fool of hope; is no more emaciated by envy, inflamed by anger, emasculated by tenderness, or depressed by grief; but walks on calmly through the tumults or the privacies of life, as the sun pursues alike his course through the calm or the stormy sky.

He enumerated many examples of heroes immovable by pain or pleasure, who looked with indifference on those modes or accidents to which the vulgar give the names of good and evil. He exhorted his hearers to lay aside their prejudices, and arm themselves against the shafts of malice or misfortune, by invulnerable patience; concluding, that this state only was happiness, and that this happiness was in every one's power.

Rasselas listened to him with the veneration due to the instructions of a superiour being, and, waiting for him at the door, humbly implored the liberty of visiting so great a master of true wisdom. The lecturer hesitated a moment, when Rasselas put a purse of gold into his hand, which he received with a mixture of joy and wonder.

'I have found, said the prince, at his return to Imlac, a man who can teach all that is necessary to be known, who, from the unshaken throne of rational fortitude, looks down on the scenes of life changing beneath him. He speaks, and attention watches his lips. He reasons, and conviction closes his periods.[69] This man shall be my future guide: I will learn his doctrines, and imitate his life.'

'Be not too hasty, said Imlac, to trust, or to admire, the teachers of morality: they discourse like angels, but they live like men.'

Rasselas, who could not conceive how any man could

reason so forcibly without feeling the cogency of his own arguments, paid his visit in a few days, and was denied admission. He had now learned the power of money, and made his way by a piece of gold to the inner apartment, where he found the philosopher in a room half darkened, with his eyes misty, and his face pale. 'Sir, said he, you are come at a time when all human friendship is useless; what I suffer cannot be remedied, what I have lost cannot be supplied.[70] My daughter, my only daughter, from whose tenderness I expected all the comforts of my age, died last night of a fever. My views, my purposes, my hopes are at an end: I am now a lonely being disunited from society.'

'Sir, said the prince, mortality is an event by which a wise man can never be surprised: we know that death is always near, and it should therefore always be expected.' 'Young man, answered the philosopher, you speak like one that has never felt the pangs of separation.' 'Have you then forgot the precepts, said Rasselas, which you so powerfully enforced? Has wisdom no strength to arm the heart against calamity? Consider, that external things are naturally variable, but truth and reason are always the same.' 'What comfort, said the mourner, can truth and reason afford me? of what effect are they now, but to tell me, that my daughter will not be restored?'

The prince, whose humanity would not suffer him to insult misery with reproof, went away convinced of the emptiness of rhetorical sound, and the inefficacy of polished periods and studied sentences.

CHAPTER XIX

A Glimpse of pastoral life

HE was still eager upon the same inquiry; and, having heard of a hermit, that lived near the lowest cataract of the Nile, and filled the whole country with the fame of his sanctity, resolved to visit his retreat, and inquire whether that felicity, which publick life could not afford, was to be found in solitude; and whether a man, whose age and virtue made him venerable, could teach any peculiar art of shunning evils, or enduring them.

Imlac and the princess agreed to accompany him, and, after the necessary preparations, they began their journey. Their way lay through fields, where shepherds tended their flocks, and the lambs were playing upon the pasture. 'This, said the poet, is the life which has been often celebrated for its innocence and quiet: let us pass the heat of the day among the shepherds' tents, and know whether all our searches are not to terminate in pastoral simplicity.'

The proposal pleased them, and they induced the shepherds, by small presents and familiar questions, to tell their opinion of their own state: they were so rude[71] and ignorant, so little able to compare the good with the evil of the occupation, and so indistinct in their narratives and descriptions, that very little could be learned from them. But it was evident that their hearts were cankered with discontent; that they considered themselves as condemned to labour for the luxury of the rich, and looked up with stupid malevolence toward those that were placed above them.

The princess pronounced with vehemence, that she would never suffer these envious savages to be her companions, and that she should not soon be desirous of seeing any more specimens of rustick happiness; but could not believe that all the accounts of primeval pleasures were fabulous, and was yet in doubt whether life had any thing that could be justly preferred to the placid gratifications of fields and woods. She hoped that the time would come, when, with a few virtuous and elegant companions, she should gather flowers planted by her own hand, fondle the lambs of her own ewe, and listen, without care, among brooks and breezes, to one of her maidens reading in the shade.[72]

CHAPTER XX

The danger of prosperity

On the next day they continued their journey, till the heat compelled them to look round for shelter. At a small distance they saw a thick wood, which they no sooner entered than they perceived that they were approaching the habitations of men. The shrubs were diligently cut away to open walks where the shades were darkest; the boughs of opposite trees were artificially interwoven; seats of flowery turf were raised in vacant spaces, and a rivulet, that wantoned along the side of a winding path, had its banks sometimes opened into small basons,[73] and its stream sometimes obstructed by little mounds of stone heaped together to increase its murmurs.

They passed slowly through the wood, delighted with such unexpected accommodations, and entertained each other with conjecturing what, or who, he could be, that, in those rude and unfrequented regions, had leisure and art for such harmless luxury.

As they advanced, they heard the sound of musick, and saw youths and virgins dancing in the grove; and, going still further, beheld a stately palace built upon a hill surrounded with woods. The laws of eastern hospitality allowed them to enter, and the master welcomed them like a man liberal and wealthy.

He was skilful enough in appearances soon to discern that they were no common guests, and spread his table with magnificence. The eloquence of Imlac caught his attention, and the lofty courtesy of the princess excited his respect. When they offered[74] to depart he entreated their stay, and was the next day still more unwilling to dismiss them than before. They were easily persuaded to stop, and civility grew up in time to freedom and confidence.

The prince now saw all the domesticks cheerful, and all

the face of nature smiling round the place, and could not forbear to hope that he should find here what he was seeking; but when he was congratulating the master upon his possessions, he answered with a sigh, 'My condition has indeed the appearance of happiness, but appearances are delusive. My prosperity puts my life in danger; the Bassa[75] of Egypt is my enemy, incensed only by my wealth and popularity. I have been hitherto protected against him by the princes of the country; but, as the favour of the great is uncertain, I know not how soon my defenders may be persuaded to share the plunder with the Bassa. I have sent my treasures into a distant country, and, upon the first alarm, am prepared to follow them. Then will my enemies riot[76] in my mansion, and enjoy the gardens which I have planted.'

They all joined in lamenting his danger, and deprecating his exile; and the princess was so much disturbed with the tumult of grief and indignation, that she retired to her apartment. They continued with their kind inviter a few days longer, and then went forward to find the hermit.

CHAPTER XXI

The happiness of solitude. The hermit's history

THEY came on the third day, by the direction of the peasants, to the hermit's cell: it was a cavern in the side of a mountain, over-shadowed with palm-trees; at such a distance from the cataract, that nothing more was heard than a gentle uniform murmur, such as composed the mind to pensive meditation, especially when it was assisted by the wind whistling among the branches. The first rude essay of nature had been so much improved by human labour, that the cave contained several apartments, appropriated to different uses, and often afforded lodging to travellers, whom darkness or tempests happened to overtake.

The hermit sat on a bench at the door, to enjoy the coolness of the evening. On one side lay a book with pens and papers, on the other mechanical instruments of various kinds. As they approached him unregarded, the princess observed that he had not the countenance of a man that had found, or could teach, the way to happiness.

They saluted him with great respect, which he repaid like a man not unaccustomed to the forms of courts. 'My children, said he, if you have lost your way, you shall be willingly supplied with such conveniencies for the night as this cavern will afford. I have all that nature requires, and you will not expect delicacies in a hermit's cell.'

They thanked him, and, entering, were pleased with the neatness and regularity of the place. The hermit set flesh and wine before them, though he fed only upon fruits and water. His discourse was cheerful without levity, and pious without enthusiasm.[77] He soon gained the esteem of his guests, and the princess repented of her hasty censure.

At last Imlac began thus: 'I do not now wonder that your reputation is so far extended; we have heard at Cairo of your wisdom, and came hither to implore your direction for this young man and maiden in the *choice of life.*'

'To him that lives well, answered the hermit, every form of life is good; nor can I give any other rule for choice, than to remove from all apparent evil.'

'He will remove most certainly from evil, said the prince, who shall devote himself to that solitude which you have recommended by your example.'

'I have indeed lived fifteen years in solitude, said the hermit, but have no desire that my example should gain any imitators. In my youth I professed arms, and was raised by degrees to the highest military rank. I have traversed wide countries at the head of my troops, and seen many battles and sieges. At last, being disgusted by the preferment of a younger officer, and feeling that my vigour was beginning to decay, I resolved to close my life in peace, having found the world full of snares, discord, and misery. I had once escaped from the pursuit of the enemy by the shelter of this cavern, and therefore chose it for my final residence. I employed artificers to form it into chambers, and stored it with all that I was likely to want.

'For some time after my retreat, I rejoiced like a tempest-beaten sailor at his entrance into the harbour, being delighted with the sudden change of the noise and hurry of war, to stillness and repose. When the pleasure of novelty went away, I employed my hours in examining the plants which grow in the valley, and the minerals which I collected from the rocks. But that inquiry is now grown tasteless and irksome. I have been for some time unsettled and distracted: my mind is disturbed with a thousand perplexities of doubt, and vanities of imagination, which hourly prevail upon me, because I have no opportunities of relaxation or diversion. I am sometimes ashamed to think that I could not secure myself from vice, but by retiring from the exercise of virtue, and begin to suspect that I was rather impelled by resentment, than led by devotion, into solitude. My fancy riots in scenes of folly, and I lament that I have lost so much, and have gained so little. In solitude, if I escape the example of bad men, I want likewise the counsel and conversation of the good. I have been long comparing the evils with the advantages of society, and resolve to return into the world to morrow. The life of a solitary man will be certainly miserable, but not certainly devout.'

They heard his resolution with surprise, but, after a short pause, offered to conduct him to Cairo. He dug up a considerable treasure which he had hid among the rocks, and accompanied them to the city, on which, as he approached it, he gazed with rapture.

CHAPTER XXII

The happiness of a life led according to nature[78]

RASSELAS went often to an assembly of learned men, who met at stated times to unbend their minds, and compare their opinions. Their manners were somewhat coarse, but their conversation was instructive, and their disputations acute, though sometimes too violent, and often continued till neither controvertist remembered upon what question they began. Some faults were almost general among them: every one was desirous to dictate to the rest, and every one was pleased to hear the genius or knowledge of another depreciated.

In this assembly Rasselas was relating his interview with the hermit, and the wonder with which he heard him censure a course of life which he had so deliberately chosen, and so laudably followed. The sentiments of the hearers were various. Some were of opinion, that the folly of his choice had been justly punished by condemnation to perpetual perseverance.[79] One of the youngest among them, with great vehemence, pronounced him an hypocrite. Some talked of the right of society to the labour of individuals, and considered retirement as a desertion of duty. Others readily allowed, that there was a time when the claims of the publick were satisfied, and when a man might properly sequester himself, to review his life, and purify his heart.

One, who appeared more affected with the narrative than the rest, thought it likely, that the hermit would, in a few years, go back to his retreat, and, perhaps, if shame did not restrain, or death intercept him, return once more from his retreat into the world: 'For the hope of happiness, said he, is so strongly impressed, that the longest experience is not able to efface it. Of the present state, whatever it be, we feel, and are forced to confess, the misery, yet, when the same state is again at a distance, imagination paints it as desirable. But the time will surely come, when desire will be no longer our torment, and no man shall be wretched but by his own fault.'

'This, said a philosopher, who had heard him with tokens of great impatience, is the present condition of a wise man. The time is already come, when none are wretched but by their own fault. Nothing is more idle, than to inquire after happiness, which nature has kindly placed within our reach. The way to be happy is to live according

to nature, in obedience to that universal and unalterable
law with which every heart is originally impressed; which
is not written on it by precept, but engraven by destiny,
not instilled by education, but infused at our nativity. He
that lives according to nature will suffer nothing from the
delusions of hope, or importunities of desire: he will receive and reject with equability of temper; and act or suffer
as the reason of things shall alternately prescribe. Other
men may amuse themselves with subtle definitions, or in-
tricate raciocination. Let them learn to be wise by easier
means: let them observe the hind of the forest, and the
linnet of the grove: let them consider the life of animals,
whose motions are regulated by instinct; they obey their
guide and are happy. Let us therefore, at length, cease to
dispute, and learn to live; throw away the incumbrance of
precepts, which they who utter them with so much pride
and pomp do not understand, and carry with us this simple
and intelligible maxim, That deviation from nature is deviation from happiness.'

When he had spoken, he looked round him with a placid
air, and enjoyed the consciousness of his own beneficence.
'Sir, said the prince, with great modesty, as I, like all the
rest of mankind, am desirous of felicity, my closest attention has been fixed upon your discourse: I doubt not the
truth of a position which a man so learned has so con-
fidently advanced. Let me only know what it is to live
according to nature.'

'When I find young men so humble and so docile, said
the philosopher, I can deny them no information which my
studies have enabled me to afford. To live according to
nature, is to act always with due regard to the fitness
arising from the relations and qualities of causes and
effects; to concur with the great and unchangeable scheme
of universal felicity; to co-operate with the general disposition and tendency of the present system of things.'

The prince soon found that this was one of the sages
whom he should understand less as he heard him longer.
He therefore bowed and was silent, and the philosopher,

supposing him satisfied, and the rest vanquished, rose up and departed with the air of a man that had co-operated with the present system.

CHAPTER XXIII

The prince and his sister divide between them the work of observation

RASSELAS returned home full of reflexions, doubtful how to direct his future steps. Of the way to happiness he found the learned and simple equally ignorant; but, as he was yet young,[80] he flattered himself that he had time remaining for more experiments, and further inquiries. He communicated to Imlac his observations and his doubts, but was answered by him with new doubts, and remarks that gave him no comfort. He therefore discoursed more frequently and freely with his sister, who had yet the same hope with himself, and always assisted him to give some reason why, though he had been hitherto frustrated, he might succeed at last.

'We have hitherto, said she, known but little of the world: we have never yet been either great or mean. In our own country, though we had royalty, we had no power, and in this we have not yet seen the private recesses of domestick peace. Imlac favours not our search, lest we should in time find him mistaken. We will divide the task between us: you shall try what is to be found in the splendour of courts, and I will range the shades of humbler life. Perhaps command and authority may be the supreme blessings, as they afford most opportunities of doing good: or, perhaps, what this world can give may be found in the modest habitations of middle fortune; too low for great designs, and too high for penury and distress.'

CHAPTER XXIV

The prince examines the happiness of high stations

RASSELAS applauded the design, and appeared next day
with a splendid retinue at the court of the Bassa. He was
soon distinguished for his magnificence, and admitted, as a
prince whose curiosity had brought him from distant
countries, to an intimacy with the great officers, and frequent conversation with the Bassa himself.

He was at first inclined to believe, that the man must be
pleased with his own condition, whom all approached with
reverence, and heard with obedience, and who had the
power to extend his edicts to a whole kingdom. 'There can
be no pleasure, said he, equal to that of feeling at once the
joy of thousands all made happy by wise administration.
Yet, since, by the law of subordination, this sublime delight
can be in one nation but the lot of one, it is surely reasonable to think that there is some satisfaction more popular[81]
and accessible, and that millions can hardly be subjected to
the will of a single man, only to fill his particular breast
with incommunicable content.'

These thoughts were often in his mind, and he found no
solution of the difficulty. But as presents and civilities
gained him more familiarity, he found that almost every
man who stood high in employment hated all the rest, and
was hated by them, and that their lives were a continual
succession of plots and detections, stratagems and escapes,
faction and treachery. Many of those, who surrounded the
Bassa, were sent only to watch and report his conduct;
every tongue was muttering censure and every eye was
searching for a fault.

At last the letters of revocation arrived, the Bassa was
carried in chains to Constantinople, and his name was
mentioned no more.

'What are we now to think of the prerogatives of power,

said Rasselas to his sister; is it without any efficacy to good? or, is the subordinate degree only dangerous, and the supreme safe and glorious? Is the Sultan the only happy man in his dominions? or, is the Sultan himself subject to the torments of suspicion, and the dread of enemies?'

In a short time the second Bassa was deposed. The Sultan, that had advanced him, was murdered by the Janisaries,[82] and his successor had other views and different favourites.

CHAPTER XXV

The princess pursues her inquiry with more diligence than success

THE princess, in the mean time, insinuated herself into many families; for there are few doors, through which liberality, joined with good humour, cannot find its way. The daughters of many houses were airy[83] and cheerful, but Nekayah had been too long accustomed to the conversation of Imlac and her brother to be much pleased with childish levity and prattle which had no meaning. She found their thoughts narrow, their wishes low, and their merriment often artificial. Their pleasures, poor as they were, could not be preserved pure, but were embittered by petty competitions and worthless emulation. They were always jealous of the beauty of each other; of a quality to which solicitude can add nothing, and from which detraction can take nothing away. Many were in love with triflers like themselves, and many fancied that they were in love when in truth they were only idle. Their affection was seldom fixed on sense or virtue, and therefore seldom ended but in vexation. Their grief, however, like their joy, was transient; every thing floated in their mind unconnected with the past or future, so that one desire easily gave way to another, as a second stone cast into the water effaces and confounds the circles of the first.

With these girls she played as with inoffensive animals, and found them proud of her countenance,[84] and weary of her company.

But her purpose was to examine more deeply, and her affability easily persuaded the hearts that were swelling with sorrow to discharge their secrets in her ear: and those whom hope flattered, or prosperity delighted, often courted her to partake their pleasures.

The princess and her brother commonly met in the evening in a private summer-house on the bank of the Nile, and related to each other the occurrences of the day. As they were sitting together, the princess cast her eyes upon the river that flowed before her. 'Answer, said she, great father of waters, thou that rollest thy floods through eighty nations, to the invocations of the daughter of thy native king. Tell me if thou waterest, through all thy course, a single habitation from which thou dost not hear the murmurs of complaint?'

'You are then, said Rasselas, not more successful in private houses than I have been in courts.' 'I have, since the last partition of our provinces,[85] said the princess, enabled myself to enter familiarly into many families, where there was the fairest show of prosperity and peace, and know not one house that is not haunted by some fury that destroys its quiet.

'I did not seek ease among the poor, because I concluded that there it could not be found. But I saw many poor whom I had supposed to live in affluence. Poverty has, in large cities, very different appearances: it is often concealed in splendour, and often in extravagance. It is the care of a very great part of mankind to conceal their indigence from the rest: they support themselves by temporary expedients, and every day is lost in contriving for the morrow.

'This, however, was an evil, which, though frequent, I saw with less pain, because I could relieve it. Yet some have refused my bounties; more offended with my quickness to

detect their wants, than pleased with my readiness to succour them: and others, whose exigencies compelled them
to admit my kindness, have never been able to forgive their
benefactress. Many, however, have been sincerely grateful
without the ostentation of gratitude, or the hope of other
favours.'

CHAPTER XXVI

The princess continues her remarks upon private life

NEKAYAH perceiving her brother's attention fixed, proceeded in her narrative.

'In families, where there is or is not poverty, there is
commonly discord: if a kingdom be, as Imlac tells us, a
great family, a family likewise is a little kingdom, torn with
factions and exposed to revolutions. An unpractised ob-
server expects the love of parents and children to be constant and equal; but this kindness seldom continues beyond
the years of infancy: in a short time the children become
rivals to their parents. Benefits are allayed[86] by reproaches,
and gratitude debased by envy.

'Parents and children seldom act in concert: each child
endeavours to appropriate the esteem or fondness of the
parents, and the parents, with yet less temptation, betray
each other to their children; thus some place their confidence in the father, and some in the mother, and, by degrees,
the house is filled with artifices and feuds.

'The opinions of children and parents, of the young and
the old, are naturally opposite, by the contrary effects of
hope and despondence, of expectation and experience,
without crime or folly on either side. The colours of life in
youth and age appear different, as the face of nature in
spring and winter. And how can children credit the asser-
tions of parents, which their own eyes show them to be
false?

'Few parents act in such a manner as much to enforce their maxims by the credit[87] of their lives. The old man trusts wholly to slow contrivance and gradual progression: the youth expects to force his way by genius, vigour, and precipitance. The old man pays regard to riches, and the youth reverences virtue. The old man deifies prudence: the youth commits himself to magnanimity and chance. The young man, who intends no ill, believes that none is intended, and therefore acts with openness and candour:[88] but his father, having suffered the injuries of fraud, is impelled to suspect, and too often allured to practise it.[89] Age looks with anger on the temerity of youth, and youth with contempt on the scrupulosity of age. Thus parents and children, for the greatest part, live on to love less and less: and, if those whom nature has thus closely united are the torments of each other, where shall we look for tenderness and consolation?'

'Surely, said the prince, you must have been unfortunate in your choice of acquaintance: I am unwilling to believe, that the most tender of all relations is thus impeded in its effects by natural necessity.'

'Domestick discord, answered she, is not inevitably and fatally necessary; but yet is not easily avoided. We seldom see that a whole family is virtuous: the good and evil cannot well agree; and the evil can yet less agree with one another: even the virtuous fall sometimes to variance, when their virtues are of different kinds, and tending to extremes. In general, those parents have most reverence who most deserve it: for he that lives well cannot be despised.

'Many other evils infest private life. Some are the slaves of servants whom they have trusted with their affairs. Some are kept in continual anxiety to the caprice of rich relations, whom they cannot please, and dare not offend. Some husbands are imperious, and some wives perverse: and, as it is always more easy to do evil than good, though the wisdom or virtue of one can very rarely make many happy, the folly or vice of one may often make many miserable.'

'If such be the general effect of marriage, said the prince,

I shall, for the future, think it dangerous to connect my interest with that of another, lest I should be unhappy by my partner's fault.'

'I have met, said the princess, with many who live single for that reason; but I never found that their prudence ought to raise envy. They dream away their time without friendship, without fondness, and are driven to rid themselves of the day, for which they have no use, by childish amusements, or vicious delights. They act as beings under the constant sense of some known inferiority, that fills their minds with rancour, and their tongues with censure. They are peevish at home, and malevolent abroad; and, as the outlaws of human nature, make it their business and their pleasure to disturb that society which debars them from its privileges. To live without feeling or exciting sympathy, to be fortunate without adding to the felicity of others, or afflicted without tasting the balm of pity, is a state more gloomy than solitude: it is not retreat but exclusion from mankind. Marriage has many pains, but celibacy has no pleasures.'

'What then is to be done? said Rasselas; the more we inquire, the less we can resolve. Surely he is most likely to please himself that has no other inclination to regard.'

CHAPTER XXVII

Disquisition upon greatness

THE conversation had a short pause. The prince, having considered his sister's observations, told her, that she had surveyed life with prejudice, and supposed misery where she did not find it. 'Your narrative, says he, throws yet a darker gloom upon the prospects of futurity: the predictions of Imlac were but faint sketches of the evils painted by Nekayah. I have been lately convinced that quiet is not the daughter of grandeur, or of power: that her presence is not to be bought by wealth, nor enforced by conquest. It is evident, that as any man acts in a wider compass, he must be more exposed to opposition from enmity or miscarriage from chance; whoever has many to please or to govern, must use the ministry of many agents, some of whom will be wicked, and some ignorant; by some he will be misled, and by others betrayed. If he gratifies one he will offend another: those that are not favoured will think themselves injured; and, since favours can be conferred but upon few, the greater number will be always discontented.'

'The discontent, said the princess, which is thus unreasonable, I hope that I shall always have spirit to despise, and you, power to repress.'

'Discontent, answered Rasselas, will not always be without reason under the most just or vigilant administration of publick affairs. None, however attentive, can always discover that merit which indigence or faction may happen to obscure; and none, however powerful, can always reward it. Yet, he that sees inferiour desert advanced above him, will naturally impute that preference to partiality or caprice; and, indeed, it can scarcely be hoped that any man, however magnanimous by nature, or exalted by condition, will be able to persist for ever in fixed and inexorable justice of distribution: he will sometimes indulge his own affections, and sometimes those of his favourites; he will permit some to please him who can never serve him; he will discover in those whom he loves qualities which in reality they do not possess; and to those, from whom he receives pleasure, he will in his turn endeavour to give it. Thus will recommendations sometimes prevail which were purchased by money, or by the more destructive bribery of flattery and servility.

'He that has much to do will do something wrong, and of that wrong must suffer the consequences; and, if it were possible that he should always act rightly, yet when such numbers are to judge of his conduct, the bad will censure and obstruct him by malevolence, and the good sometimes by mistake.

'The highest stations cannot therefore hope to be the

abodes of happiness, which I would willingly believe to have fled from thrones and palaces to seats of humble privacy and placid obscurity. For what can hinder the satisfaction, or intercept the expectations, of him whose abilities are adequate to his employments, who sees with his own eyes the whole circuit of his influence, who chooses by his own knowledge all whom he trusts, and whom none are tempted to deceive by hope or fear? Surely he has nothing to do but to love and to be loved, to be virtuous and to be happy.'

'Whether perfect happiness would be procured by perfect goodness, said Nekayah, this world will never afford an opportunity of deciding. But this, at least, may be maintained, that we do not always find visible happiness in proportion to visible virtue. All natural and almost all political evils, are incident alike to the bad and good: they are confounded in the misery of a famine, and not much distinguished in the fury of a faction; they sink together in a tempest, and are driven together from their country by invaders. All that virtue can afford is quietness of conscience, a steady prospect of a happier state; this may enable us to endure calamity with patience; but remember that patience must suppose pain.'

CHAPTER XXVIII

Rasselas and Nekayah continue their conversation

'DEAR princess, said Rasselas, you fall into the common errours of exaggeratory declamation, by producing, in a familiar disquisition, examples of national calamities, and scenes of extensive misery, which are found in books rather than in the world, and which, as they are horrid, are ordained to be rare. Let us not imagine evils which we do not feel, nor injure life by misrepresentations. I cannot bear that querulous eloquence which threatens every city with a siege like that of Jerusalem,[90] that makes famine attend on every flight of locusts, and suspends pestilence on the wing of every blast that issues from the south.

'On necessary and inevitable evils, which overwhelm kingdoms at once, all disputation is vain: when they happen they must be endured. But it is evident, that these bursts of universal distress are more dreaded than felt: thousands and ten thousands flourish in youth, and wither in age, without the knowledge of any other than domestick evils, and share the same pleasures and vexations whether their kings are mild or cruel, whether the armies of their country pursue their enemies, or retreat before them. While courts are disturbed with intestine competitions, and ambassadours are negotiating in foreign countries, the smith still plies his anvil, and the husbandman drives his plow forward; the necessaries of life are required and obtained, and the successive business of the seasons continues to make its wonted revolutions.

'Let us cease to consider what, perhaps, may never happen, and what, when it shall happen, will laugh at human speculation. We will not endeavour to modify the motions of the elements, or to fix the destiny of kingdoms. It is our business to consider what beings like us may perform; each labouring for his own happiness, by promoting within his circle, however narrow, the happiness of others.

'Marriage is evidently the dictate of nature; men and women were made to be companions of each other, and therefore I cannot be persuaded but that marriage is one of the means of happiness.'

'I know not, said the princess, whether marriage be more than one of the innumerable modes of human misery. When I see and reckon the various forms of connubial infelicity, the unexpected causes of lasting discord, the diversities of temper, the oppositions of opinion, the rude collisions of contrary desire where both are urged by violent impulses, the obstinate contests of disagreeing virtues, where both are supported by consciousness of good intention, I am sometimes disposed to think with the severer casuists of most nations, that marriage is rather permitted than approved, and that none, but by the instigation of a passion too much indulged, entangle themselves with indissoluble compacts.'

'You seem to forget, replied Rasselas, that you have, even now, represented celibacy as less happy than marriage. Both conditions may be bad, but they cannot both be worst. Thus it happens when wrong opinions are entertained, that they mutually destroy each other, and leave the mind open to truth.'

'I did not expect, answered the princess, to hear that imputed to falsehood which is the consequence only of frailty. To the mind, as to the eye, it is difficult to compare with exactness objects vast in their extent, and various in their parts. Where we see or conceive the whole at once we readily note the discriminations and decide the preference: but of two systems, of which neither can be surveyed by any human being in its full compass of magnitude and multiplicity of complication, where is the wonder, that judging of the whole by parts, I am alternately affected by one and the other as either presses on my memory or fancy? We differ from ourselves just as we differ from each other, when we see only part of the question, as in the multifarious relations of politicks and morality: but when we perceive the whole at once, as in numerical computations, all agree in one judgment, and none ever varies his opinion.'

'Let us not add, said the prince, to the other evils of life, the bitterness of controversy, nor endeavour to vie with each other in subtilties of argument. We are employed in a search, of which both are equally to enjoy the success, or suffer by the miscarriage. It is therefore fit that we assist each other. You surely conclude too hastily from the infelicity of marriage against its institution; will not the misery of life prove equally that life cannot be the gift of heaven? The world must be peopled by marriage, or peopled without it.'

'How the world is to be peopled, returned Nekayah, is not my care, and needs not be yours. I see no danger that the present generation should omit to leave successors behind them: we are not now inquiring for the world, but for ourselves.'

CHAPTER XXIX

The debate on marriage continued

'THE good of the whole, says Rasselas, is the same with the good of all its parts. If marriage be best for mankind it must be evidently best for individuals, or a permanent and necessary duty must be the cause of evil, and some must be inevitably sacrificed to the convenience of others. In the estimate which you have made of the two states, it appears that the incommodities of a single life are, in a great measure, necessary and certain, but those of the conjugal state accidental and avoidable.

'I cannot forbear to flatter myself that prudence and benevolence will make marriage happy. The general folly of mankind is the cause of general complaint. What can be expected but disappointment and repentance from a choice made in the immaturity of youth, in the ardour of desire, without judgment, without foresight, without inquiry after conformity of opinions, similarity of manners, rectitude of judgment, or purity of sentiment.

'Such is the common process of marriage. A youth and maiden meeting by chance, or brought together by artifice, exchange glances, reciprocate civilities, go home, and dream of one another. Having little to divert attention, or diversify thought, they find themselves uneasy when they are apart, and therefore conclude that they shall be happy together. They marry, and discover what nothing but voluntary blindness had before concealed; they wear out life in altercations, and charge nature with cruelty.

'From those early marriages proceeds likewise the rivalry of parents and children: the son is eager to enjoy the world before the father is willing to forsake it, and there is hardly room at once for two generations. The daughter begins to bloom before the mother can be content to fade, and neither can forbear to wish for the absence of the other.[91]

'Surely all these evils may be avoided by that deliberation and delay which prudence prescribes to irrevocable choice. In the variety and jollity of youthful pleasures life may be well enough supported without the help of a partner. Longer time will increase experience, and wider views will allow better opportunities of inquiry and selection: one advantage, at least, will be certain; the parents will be visibly older than their children.'

'What reason cannot collect,[92] said Nekayah, and what experiment has not yet taught, can be known only from the report of others. I have been told that late marriages are not eminently happy. This is a question too important to be neglected, and I have often proposed it to those, whose accuracy of remark, and comprehensiveness of knowledge, made their suffrages[93] worthy of regard. They have generally determined, that it is dangerous for a man and woman to suspend their fate upon each other, at a time when opinions are fixed, and habits are established; when friendships have been contracted on both sides, when life has been planned into method, and the mind has long enjoyed the contemplation of its own prospects.

'It is scarcely possible that two travelling through the world under the conduct of chance, should have been both directed to the same path, and it will not often happen that either will quit the track which custom has made pleasing. When the desultory levity of youth has settled into regularity, it is soon succeeded by pride ashamed to yield, or obstinacy delighting to contend. And even though mutual esteem produces mutual desire to please, time itself, as it modifies unchangeably the external mien, determines likewise the direction of the passions, and gives an inflexible rigidity to the manners. Long customs are not easily broken: he that attempts to change the course of his own life, very often labours in vain; and how shall we do that for others which we are seldom able to do for ourselves?'

The History of Rasselas

'But surely, interposed the prince, you suppose the chief
motive of choice forgotten or neglected. Whenever I shall
seek a wife, it shall be my first question, whether she be
willing to be led by reason?'

'Thus it is, said Nekayah, that philosophers are deceived.
There are a thousand familiar disputes which reason never
can decide; questions that elude investigation, and make
logick ridiculous; cases where something must be done,
and where little can be said. Consider the state of mankind, and inquire how few can be supposed to act upon
any occasions, whether small or great, with all the reasons
of action present to their minds. Wretched would be the
pair above all names of wretchedness, who should be
doomed to adjust by reason every morning all the minute
detail of a domestick day.

'Those who marry at an advanced age, will probably
escape the encroachments of their children; but, in diminution of this advantage, they will be likely to leave them,
ignorant and helpless, to a guardian's mercy: or, if that
should not happen, they must at least go out of the world
before they see those whom they love best either wise or
great.

'From their children, if they have less to fear, they have
less also to hope, and they lose, without equivalent, the
joys of early love, and the convenience of uniting with
manners pliant, and minds susceptible of new impressions,
which might wear away their dissimilitudes by long cohabi-
tation, as soft bodies, by continual attrition, conform their
surfaces to each other.

'I believe it will be found that those who marry late are
best pleased with their children, and those who marry
early with their partners.'

'The union of these two affections, said Rasselas, would
produce all that could be wished. Perhaps there is a time
when marriage might unite them, a time neither too early
for the father, nor too late for the husband.'

'Every hour, answered the princess, confirms my prejudice in favour of the position so often uttered by the

mouth of Imlac, "That nature sets her gifts on the right hand and on the left." Those conditions, which flatter hope and attract desire, are so constituted, that, as we approach one, we recede from another. There are goods so opposed that we cannot seize both, but, by too much prudence, may pass between them at too great a distance to reach either. This is often the fate of long consideration; he does nothing who endeavours to do more than is allowed to humanity. Flatter not yourself with contrarieties of pleasure. Of the blessings set before you make your choice, and be content. No man can taste the fruits of autumn while he is delighting his scent[94] with the flowers of the spring: no man can, at the same time, fill his cup from the source and from the mouth of the Nile.'

CHAPTER XXX

Imlac enters, and changes the conversation

HERE Imlac entered, and interrupted them. 'Imlac, said Rasselas, I have been taking from the princess the dismal history of private life, and am almost discouraged from further search.'

'It seems to me, said Imlac, that while you are making the choice of life, you neglect to live. You wander about a single city, which, however large and diversified, can now afford few novelties, and forget that you are in a country, famous among the earliest monarchies for the power and wisdom of its inhabitants; a country where the sciences first dawned that illuminate the world, and beyond which the arts cannot be traced of civil[95] society or domestick life.

'The old Egyptians have left behind them monuments of industry and power before which all European magnificence is confessed to fade away. The ruins of their architecture are the schools of modern builders, and from the wonders which time has spared we may conjecture, though uncertainly, what it has destroyed.'

'My curiosity," said Rasselas, does not very strongly lead me to survey piles of stone, or mounds of earth; my business is with man. I came hither not to measure fragments of temples, or trace choaked aqueducts, but to look upon the various scenes of the present world.'

'The things that are now before us, said the princess, require attention, and deserve it. What have I to do with the heroes or the monuments of ancient times? with times which never can return, and heroes, whose form of life was different from all that the present condition of mankind requires or allows.'

'To know any thing, returned the poet, we must know its effects; to see men we must see their works, that we may learn what reason has dictated, or passion has incited, and find what are the most powerful motives of action. To judge rightly of the present we must oppose it to the past; for all judgment is comparative, and of the future nothing can be known. The truth is, that no mind is much employed upon the present: recollection and anticipation fill up almost all our moments. Our passions are joy and grief, love and hatred, hope and fear. Of joy and grief the past is the object, and the future of hope and fear; even love and hatred respect the past, for the cause must have been before the effect.

'The present state of things is the consequence of the former, and it is natural to inquire what were the sources of the good that we enjoy, or of the evil that we suffer. If we act only for ourselves, to neglect the study of history is not prudent: if we are entrusted with the care of others, it is not just. Ignorance, when it is voluntary, is criminal; and he may properly be charged with evil who refused to learn how he might prevent it.

'There is no part of history so generally useful as that which relates the progress of the human mind, the gradual improvement of reason, the successive advances of science, the vicissitudes of learning and ignorance, which are the light and darkness of thinking beings, the extinction and resuscitation of arts, and all the revolutions of the intellectual world. If accounts of battles and invasions are peculiarly the business of princes, the useful or elegant arts are not to be neglected; those who have kingdoms to govern, have understandings to cultivate.

'Example is always more efficacious than precept. A soldier is formed in war, and a painter must copy pictures. In this, contemplative life has the advantage: great actions are seldom seen, but the labours of art are always at hand for those who desire to know what art has been able to perform.

'When the eye or the imagination is struck with any un-common work the next transition of an active mind is to the means by which it was performed. Here begins the true use of such contemplation; we enlarge our compre-hension by new ideas, and perhaps recover some art lost to mankind, or learn what is less perfectly known in our own country. At least we compare our own with former times, and either rejoice at our improvements, or, what is the first motion towards good, discover our defects.'

'I am willing, said the prince, to see all that can deserve my search.' 'And I, said the princess, shall rejoice to learn something of the manners of antiquity.'

'The most pompous[96] monument of Egyptian greatness, and one of the most bulky works of manual industry, said Imlac, are the pyramids; fabricks raised before the time of history, and of which the earliest narratives afford us only uncertain traditions. Of these the greatest is still standing, very little injured by time.'

'Let us visit them to morrow, said Nekayah. I have often heard of the pyramids, and shall not rest, till I have seen them within and without with my own eyes.'

CHAPTER XXXI

They visit the pyramids

THE resolution being thus taken, they set out the next day. They laid tents upon their camels, being resolved to stay among the pyramids till their curiosity was fully satisfied. They travelled gently, turned aside to every thing remarkable, stopped from time to time and conversed with the inhabitants, and observed the various appearances of towns ruined and inhabited, of wild and cultivated nature.

When they came to the great pyramid they were astonished at the extent of the base, and the height of the top. Imlac explained to them the principles upon which the pyramidal form was chosen for a fabrick intended to co-extend its duration with that of the world: he showed that its gradual diminution gave it such stability, as defeated all the common attacks of the elements, and could scarcely be overthrown by earthquakes themselves, the least resistible of natural violence. A concussion that should shatter the pyramid would threaten the dissolution of the continent.

They measured all its dimensions, and pitched their tents at its foot. Next day they prepared to enter its interiour apartments, and having hired the common guides climbed up to the first passage, when the favourite of the princess, looking into the cavity, stepped back and trembled. 'Pekuah, said the princess, of what art thou afraid?' 'Of the narrow entrance, answered the lady, and of the dreadful gloom. I dare not enter a place which must surely be inhabited by unquiet souls. The original possessors of these dreadful vaults will start up before us, and, perhaps, shut us in for ever.' She spoke, and threw her arms round the neck of her mistress.

'If all your fear be of apparitions, said the prince, I will promise you safety: there is no danger from the dead; he that is once buried will be seen no more.'

'That the dead are seen no more, said Imlac, I will not undertake to maintain against the concurrent and unvaried testimony of all ages, and of all nations. There is no people, rude or learned, among whom apparitions of the dead are not related and believed. This opinion, which, perhaps, prevails as far as human nature is diffused, could become universal only by its truth: those, that never heard of one another, would not have agreed in a tale which nothing but experience can make credible. That it is doubted by single cavillers can very little weaken the general evidence, and some who deny it with their tongues confess it by their fears.[97]

'Yet I do not mean to add new terrours to those which have already seized upon Pekuah. There can be no reason why spectres should haunt the pyramid more than other places, or why they should have power or will to hurt innocence and purity. Our entrance is no violation of their privileges; we can take nothing from them, how then can we offend them?'

'My dear Pekuah, said the princess, I will always go before you, and Imlac shall follow you. Remember that you are the companion of the princess of Abissinia.'

'If the princess is pleased that her servant should die, returned the lady, let her command some death less dreadful than enclosure in this horrid cavern. You know I dare not disobey you: I must go if you command me; but, if I once enter, I never shall come back.'

The princess saw that her fear was too strong for expostulation or reproof, and embracing her, told her that she should stay in the tent till their return. Pekuah was yet not satisfied, but entreated the princess not to pursue so dreadful a purpose as that of entering the recesses of the pyramid. 'Though I cannot teach courage, said Nekayah, I must not learn cowardice; nor leave at last undone what I came hither only to do.'

CHAPTER XXXII

They enter the pyramid

PEKUAH descended to the tents, and the rest entered the pyramid: they passed through the galleries, surveyed the vaults of marble, and examined the chest in which the body of the founder is supposed to have been reposited. They then sat down in one of the most spacious chambers to rest a while before they attempted to return.

'We have now, said Imlac, gratified our minds with an exact view of the greatest work of man, except the wall of China.[98]

'Of the wall it is very easy to assign the motives. It secured a wealthy and timorous nation from the incursions of Barbarians, whose unskilfulness in arts made it easier for them to supply their wants by rapine than by industry, and who from time to time poured in upon the habitations of peaceful commerce, as vultures descend upon domestick fowl. Their celerity and fierceness made the wall necessary, and their ignorance made it efficacious.

'But for the pyramids no reason has ever been given adequate to the cost and labour of the work. The narrowness of the chambers proves that it could afford no retreat from enemies, and treasures might have been reposited at far less expence with equal security. It seems to have been erected only in compliance with that hunger of imagination which preys incessantly upon life, and must be always appeased by some employment. Those who have already all that they can enjoy, must enlarge their desires.[99] He that has built for use, till use is supplied,[100] must begin to build for vanity, and extend his plan to the utmost power of human performance, that he may not be soon reduced to form another wish.

'I consider this mighty structure as a monument of the insufficiency of human enjoyments. A king, whose power is unlimited, and whose treasures surmount all real and imaginary wants, is compelled to solace, by the erection of a pyramid, the satiety of dominion and tastelessness of pleasures, and to amuse the tediousness of declining life, by seeing thousands labouring without end, and one stone, for no purpose, laid upon another. Whoever thou art, that, not content with a moderate condition, imaginest happiness in royal magnificence, and dreamest that command or riches can feed the appetite of novelty with perpetual gratifications, survey the pyramids, and confess thy folly!'

CHAPTER XXXIII

The princess meets with an unexpected misfortune

THEY rose up, and returned through the cavity at which they had entered, and the princess prepared for her favourite a long narrative of dark labyrinths, and costly rooms, and of the different impressions which the varieties of the way had made upon her. But, when they came to their train, they found every one silent and dejected: the men discovered shame and fear in their countenances, and the women were weeping in the tents.

What had happened they did not try to conjecture, but immediately inquired. 'You had scarcely entered into the pyramid, said one of the attendants, when a troop of Arabs rushed upon us: we were too few to resist them, and too slow to escape. They were about to search the tents, set us on our camels, and drive us along before them, when the approach of some Turkish horsemen put them to flight; but they seized the lady Pekuah with her two maids, and carried them away: the Turks are now pursuing them by our instigation, but I fear they will not be able to overtake them.'

The princess was overpowered with surprise and grief. Rasselas, in the first heat of his resentment, ordered his servants to follow him, and prepared to pursue the robbers with his sabre in his hand. 'Sir, said Imlac, what can you hope from violence or valour? The Arabs are mounted on horses trained to battle and retreat;[101] we have only beasts of burthen. By leaving our present station we may lose the princess, but cannot hope to regain Pekuah.'

In a short time the Turks returned, having not been able to reach the enemy. The princess burst out into new lamentations, and Rasselas could scarcely forbear to reproach them with cowardice; but Imlac was of opinion, that the escape of the Arabs was no addition to their misfortune, for, perhaps, they would have killed their captives rather than have resigned them.

CHAPTER XXXIV

They return to Cairo without Pekuah

THERE was nothing to be hoped from longer stay. They returned to Cairo repenting of their curiosity, censuring the negligence of the government, lamenting their own rashness which had neglected to procure a guard, imagining many expedients by which the loss of Pekuah might have been prevented, and resolving to do something for her recovery, though none could find any thing proper to be done.

Nekayah retired to her chamber, where her women attempted to comfort her, by telling her that all had their troubles, and that lady Pekuah had enjoyed much happiness in the world for a long time, and might reasonably expect a change of fortune. They hoped that some good would befall her wheresoever she was, and that their mistress would find another friend who might supply her place.

The princess made them no answer, and they continued the form of condolence, not much grieved in their hearts that the favourite was lost.

Next day the prince presented to the Bassa a memorial of the wrong which he had suffered, and a petition for redress. The Bassa threatened to punish the robbers, but did not attempt to catch them, nor, indeed, could any account or description be given by which he might direct the pursuit.

It soon appeared that nothing would be done by authority. Governors, being accustomed to hear of more crimes than they can punish, and more wrongs than they can redress, set themselves at ease by indiscriminate negligence, and presently forget the request when they lose sight of the petitioner.

Imlac then endeavoured to gain some intelligence by private agents. He found many who pretended to an exact knowledge of all the haunts of the Arabs, and to regular correspondence with their chiefs, and who readily undertook the recovery of Pekuah. Of these, some were furnished with money for their journey, and came back no more; some were liberally paid for accounts which a few days discovered to be false. But the princess would not suffer any means, however improbable, to be left untried. While she was doing something she kept her hope alive. As one expedient failed, another was suggested; when one messenger returned unsuccessful, another was dispatched to a different quarter.

Two months had now passed, and of Pekuah nothing had been heard; the hopes which they had endeavoured to raise in each other grew more languid, and the princess, when she saw nothing more to be tried, sunk down inconsolable in hopeless dejection. A thousand times she reproached herself with the easy compliance by which she permitted her favourite to stay behind her. 'Had not my fondness, said she, lessened my authority, Pekuah had not dared to talk of her terrours. She ought to have feared me more than spectres. A severe look would have overpowered her; a peremptory command would have compelled obedience. Why did foolish indulgence prevail upon me? Why did I not speak and refuse to hear?'

'Great princess, said Imlac, do not reproach yourself for your virtue, or consider that as blameable by which evil has accidentally been caused. Your tenderness for the timidity of Pekuah was generous and kind. When we act according to our duty, we commit the event to him by whose laws our actions are governed, and who will suffer none to be finally punished for obedience. When, in prospect of some good, whether natural or moral, we break the rules prescribed us, we withdraw from the direction of superiour wisdom, and take all consequences upon ourselves. Man cannot so far know the connexion of causes and events, as that he may venture to do wrong in order to do right. When we pursue our end by lawful means, we may always console our miscarriage by the hope of future recompense. When we consult only our own policy, and attempt to find a nearer way to good, by overleaping the settled boundaries of right and wrong, we cannot be happy even by success, because we cannot escape the consciousness of our fault; but, if we miscarry, the disappointment is irremediably embittered. How comfortless is the sorrow of him, who feels at once the pangs of guilt, and the vexation of calamity which guilt has brought upon him?

'Consider, princess, what would have been your condition, if the lady Pekuah had entreated to accompany you, and, being compelled to stay in the tents, had been carried away; or how would you have born the thought, if you had forced her into the pyramid, and she had died before you in agonies of terrour.'

'Had either happened, said Nekayah, I could not have endured life till now: I should have been tortured to madness by the remembrance of such cruelty, or must have pined away in abhorrence of myself.'

'This at least, said Imlac, is the present reward of virtuous conduct, that no unlucky consequence can oblige us to repent it.'

CHAPTER XXXV

The princess languishes for want of Pekuah

NEKAYAH, being thus reconciled to herself, found that no evil is insupportable but that which is accompanied with consciousness of wrong. She was, from that time, delivered from the violence of tempestuous sorrow, and sunk into silent pensiveness and gloomy tranquillity. She sat from morning to evening recollecting all that had been done or said by her Pekuah, treasured up with care every trifle on which Pekuah had set an accidental value, and which might recall to mind any little incident or careless conversation. The sentiments of her, whom she now expected to see no more, were treasured in her memory as rules of life, and she deliberated to no other end than to conjecture on any occasion what would have been the opinion and counsel of Pekuah.

The women, by whom she was attended, knew nothing of her real condition,[102] and therefore she could not talk to them but with caution and reserve. She began to remit her curiosity, having no great care to collect notions which she had no convenience[103] of uttering. Rasselas endeavoured first to comfort and afterwards to divert her; he hired musicians, to whom she seemed to listen, but did not hear them, and procured masters to instruct her in various arts, whose lectures, when they visited her again, were again to be repeated. She had lost her taste of pleasure and her ambition of excellence. And her mind, though forced into short excursions,[104] always recurred to the image of her friend.

Imlac was every morning earnestly enjoined to renew his inquiries, and was asked every night whether he had yet heard of Pekuah, till not being able to return the princess the answer that she desired, he was less and less willing to come into her presence. She observed his backwardness, and commanded him to attend her. 'You are not, said she, to confound impatience with resentment, or to suppose that I charge you with negligence, because I repine at your unsuccessfulness. I do not much wonder at your absence; I know that the unhappy are never pleasing, and that all naturally avoid the contagion of misery. To hear complaints is wearisome alike to the wretched and the happy; for who would cloud by adventitious grief the short gleams of gaiety which life allows us? or who, that is struggling under his own evils, will add to them the miseries of another?

'The time is at hand, when none shall be disturbed any longer by the sighs of Nekayah: my search after happiness is now at an end. I am resolved to retire from the world with all its flatteries and deceits, and will hide myself in solitude, without any other care than to compose my thoughts, and regulate my hours by a constant succession of innocent occupations, till, with a mind purified from all earthly desires, I shall enter into that state, to which all are hastening, and in which I hope again to enjoy the friendship of Pekuah.'

'Do not entangle your mind, said Imlac, by irrevocable determinations, nor increase the burthen of life by a voluntary accumulation of misery: the weariness of retirement will continue or increase when the loss of Pekuah is forgotten. That you have been deprived of one pleasure is no very good reason for rejection of the rest.'

'Since Pekuah was taken from me, said the princess, I have no pleasure to reject or to retain. She that has no one to love or trust has little to hope. She wants the radical principle of happiness. We may, perhaps, allow that what satisfaction this world can afford, must arise from the conjunction of wealth, knowledge and goodness: wealth is nothing but as it is bestowed, and knowledge nothing but as it is communicated: they must therefore be imparted to others, and to whom could I now delight to impart them? Goodness affords the only comfort which can be enjoyed

without a partner, and goodness may be practised in retirement.'

'How far solitude may admit goodness, or advance it,
I shall not, replied Imlac, dispute at present. Remember
the confession of the pious hermit. You will wish to return
into the world, when the image of your companion has left
your thoughts.' 'That time, said Nekayah, will never come.
The generous frankness, the modest obsequiousness,[105]
and the faithful secrecy of my dear Pekuah, will always
be more missed, as I shall live longer to see vice and
folly.'

'The state of a mind oppressed with a sudden calamity,
said Imlac, is like that of the fabulous inhabitants of the
new created earth, who, when the first night came upon
them, supposed that day never would return. When the
clouds of sorrow gather over us, we see nothing beyond
them, nor can imagine how they will be dispelled: yet a new
day succeeded to the night, and sorrow is never long without a dawn of ease. But they who restrain themselves from
receiving comfort, do as the savages would have done, had
they put out their eyes when it was dark. Our minds, like
our bodies, are in continual flux; something is hourly lost,
and something acquired. To lose much at once is inconvenient to either, but while the vital powers remain un-
injured, nature will find the means of reparation. Distance
has the same effect on the mind as on the eye, and while we
glide along the stream of time, whatever we leave behind us
is always lessening, and that which we approach increasing
in magnitude. Do not suffer life to stagnate; it will grow
muddy for want of motion: commit yourself again to the
current of the world; Pekuah will vanish by degrees; you
will meet in your way some other favourite, or learn to
diffuse yourself[106] in general conversation.'

'At least, said the prince, do not despair before all reme-
dies have been tried: the inquiry after the unfortunate lady
is still continued, and shall be carried on with yet greater
diligence, on condition that you will promise to wait a year
for the event, without any unalterable resolution.'

Nekayah thought this a reasonable demand, and made the promise to her brother, who had been advised by Imlac to require it. Imlac had, indeed, no great hope of regaining Pekuah, but he supposed, that if he could secure the interval of a year, the princess would be then in no danger of a cloister.

CHAPTER XXXVI

Pekuah is still remembered. The progress of sorrow

NEKAYAH, seeing that nothing was omitted for the recovery of her favourite, and having, by her promise, set her intention of retirement at a distance, began imperceptibly to return to common cares and common pleasures. She rejoiced without her own consent at the suspension of her sorrows, and sometimes caught herself with indignation in the act of turning away her mind from the remembrance of her, whom yet she resolved never to forget.

She then appointed a certain hour of the day for meditation on the merits and fondness of Pekuah, and for some weeks retired constantly at the time fixed, and returned with her eyes swollen and her countenance clouded. By degrees she grew less scrupulous, and suffered any important and pressing avocation[107] to delay the tribute of daily tears. She then yielded to less occasions; sometimes forgot what she was indeed afraid to remember, and, at last, wholly released herself from the duty of periodical affliction.

Her real love of Pekuah was yet not diminished. A thousand occurrences brought her back to memory, and a thousand wants, which nothing but the confidence of friendship can supply, made her frequently regretted. She, therefore, solicited Imlac never to desist from inquiry, and to leave no art of intelligence untried, that, at least, she might have the comfort of knowing that she did not suffer by negligence or sluggishness. 'Yet what, said she, is to be expected from our pursuit of happiness, when we find the state of life to be such, that happiness itself is the cause of misery? Why should we endeavour to attain that, of which the possession cannot be secured? I shall henceforward fear to yield my heart to excellence, however bright, or to fondness, however tender, lest I should lose again what I have lost in Pekuah.'

CHAPTER XXXVII

The princess hears news of Pekuah

IN seven months, one of the messengers, who had been sent away upon the day when the promise was drawn from the princess, returned, after many unsuccessful rambles, from the borders of Nubia, with an account that Pekuah was in the hands of an Arab chief, who possessed a castle or fortress on the extremity of Egypt. The Arab, whose revenue was plunder, was willing to restore her, with her two attendants, for two hundred ounces of gold.

The price was no subject of debate. The princess was in extasies when she heard that her favourite was alive, and might so cheaply be ransomed. She could not think of delaying for a moment Pekuah's happiness or her own, but entreated her brother to send back the messenger with the sum required. Imlac, being consulted, was not very confident of the veracity of the relator, and was still more doubtful of the Arab's faith, who might, if he were too liberally trusted, detain at once the money and the captives. He thought it dangerous to put themselves in the power of the Arab, by going into his district, and could not expect that the Rover would so much expose himself as to come into the lower country, where he might be seized by the forces of the Bassa.

It is difficult to negotiate where neither will trust. But Imlac, after some deliberation, directed the messenger to propose that Pekuah should be conducted by ten horsemen to the monastery of St Anthony,[108] which is situated in the deserts of Upper-Egypt, where she should be met by the same number, and her ransome should be paid.

That no time might be lost, as they expected that the proposal would not be refused, they immediately began their journey to the monastery; and, when they arrived, Imlac went forward with the former messenger to the Arab's fortress. Rasselas was desirous to go with them, but neither his sister nor Imlac would consent. The Arab, according to the custom of his nation, observed the laws of hospitality with great exactness to those who put themselves into his power, and, in a few days, brought Pekuah with her maids, by easy journeys, to their place appointed, where receiving the stipulated price, he restored her with great respect to liberty and her friends, and undertook to conduct them back towards Cairo beyond all danger of robbery or violence.

The princess and her favourite embraced each other with transport too violent to be expressed, and went out together to pour the tears of tenderness in secret, and exchange professions of kindness and gratitude. After a few hours they returned into the refectory of the convent, where, in the presence of the prior and his brethren, the prince required of Pekuah the history of her adventures.

CHAPTER XXXVIII

The adventures of the lady Pekuah

'At what time, and in what manner, I was forced away, said Pekuah, your servants have told you. The suddenness of the event struck me with surprise, and I was at first rather stupified than agitated with any passion of either fear or sorrow. My confusion was increased by the speed and tumult of our flight while we were followed by the Turks, who, as it seemed, soon despaired to overtake us, or were afraid of those whom they made a show of menacing.

'When the Arabs saw themselves out of danger they slackened their course, and, as I was less harassed by external violence, I began to feel more uneasiness in my mind. After some time we stopped near a spring shaded with trees in a pleasant meadow,[109] where we were set upon the ground, and offered such refreshments as our masters were partaking. I was suffered to sit with my maids apart from the rest, and none attempted to comfort or insult us. Here I first began to feel the full weight of my misery. The girls sat weeping in silence, and from time to time looked on me for succour. I knew not to what condition we were doomed, nor could conjecture where would be the place of our captivity, or whence to draw any hope of deliverance. I was in the hands of robbers and savages, and had no reason to suppose that their pity was more than their justice, or that they would forbear the gratification of any ardour of desire, or caprice of cruelty. I, however, kissed my maids, and endeavoured to pacify them by remarking, that we were yet treated with decency, and that, since we were now carried beyond pursuit, there was no danger of violence to our lives.

'When we were to be set again on horseback, my maids clung round me, and refused to be parted, but I commanded them not to irritate those who had us in their power. We travelled the remaining part of the day through an unfrequented and pathless country, and came by moonlight to the side of a hill, where the rest of the troop was stationed. Their tents were pitched, and their fires kindled, and our chief was welcomed as a man much beloved by his dependants.

'We were received into a large tent, where we found women who had attended their husbands in the expedition. They set before us the supper which they had provided, and I eat it rather to encourage my maids than to comply with any appetite of my own. When the meat was taken away they spread the carpets for repose. I was weary, and hoped to find in sleep that remission of distress which nature seldom denies. Ordering myself therefore to be undrest, I observed that the women looked very earnestly upon me, not expecting, I suppose, to see me so submissively attended. When my upper vest was taken off, they were apparently struck with the splendour of my cloaths, and one of them timorously laid her hand upon the embroidery. She then went out, and, in a short time, came back with another woman, who seemed to be of higher rank, and greater authority. She did, at her entrance, the usual act of reverence, and, taking me by the hand, placed me in a smaller tent, spread with finer carpets, where I spent the night quietly with my maids.

'In the morning, as I was sitting on the grass, the chief of the troop came towards me. I rose up to receive him, and he bowed with great respect. 'Illustrious lady, said he, my fortune is better than I had presumed to hope; I am told by my women, that I have a princess in my camp.' Sir, answered I, your women have deceived themselves and you; I am not a princess, but an unhappy stranger who intended soon to have left this country, in which I am now to be imprisoned for ever. 'Whoever, or whencesoever, you are, returned the Arab, your dress, and that of your servants, show your rank to be high, and your wealth to be great. Why should you, who can so easily procure your ransome, think yourself in danger of perpetual captivity? The purpose of my incursions is to increase my riches, or more properly to gather tribute. The sons of Ishmael[110] are the natural and hereditary lords of this part of the continent, which is usurped by late invaders, and low-born tyrants, from whom we are compelled to take by the sword what is denied to justice. The violence of war admits no distinction; the lance that is lifted at guilt and power will sometimes fall on innocence and gentleness.'

'How little, said I, did I expect that yesterday it should have fallen upon me.'

'Misfortunes, answered the Arab. should always be expected. If the eye of hostility could learn reverence or pity, excellence like yours had been exempt from injury. But the angels of affliction spread their toils alike for the virtuous and the wicked, for the mighty and the mean. Do not be disconsolate; I am not one of the lawless and cruel rovers of the desert; I know the rules of civil life: I will fix your ransome, give a pasport[111] to your messenger, and perform my stipulation with nice punctuality.'[112]

'You will easily believe that I was pleased with his courtesy; and finding that his predominant passion was desire of money, I began now to think my danger less, for I knew that no sum would be thought too great for the release of Pekuah. I told him that he should have no reason to charge me with ingratitude, if I was used with kindness, and that any ransome, which could be expected for a maid of common rank, would be paid, but that he must not persist to rate me as a princess. He said, he would consider what he should demand, and then, smiling, bowed and retired.

'Soon after the women came about me, each contending to be more officious than the other, and my maids themselves were served with reverence. We travelled onward by short journeys. On the fourth day the chief told me, that my ransome must be two hundred ounces of gold, which I not only promised him, but told him, that I would add fifty more, if I and my maids were honourably treated.

'I never knew the power of gold before. From that time I was the leader of the troop. The march of every day was longer or shorter as I commanded, and the tents were pitched where I chose to rest. We now had camels and other conveniencies for travel, my own women were always at my side, and I amused myself with observing the manners of the vagrant nations, and with viewing remains of ancient edifices with which these deserted countries appear to have been, in some distant age, lavishly embellished.

'The chief of the band was a man far from illiterate: he was able to travel by the stars or the compass, and had marked in his erratick[113] expeditions such places as are most worthy the notice of a passenger.[114] He observed to me, that buildings are always best preserved in places little frequented, and difficult of access: for, when once a country declines from its primitive splendour, the more inhabitants are left, the quicker ruin will be made. Walls supply stones more easily than quarries, and palaces and temples will be demolished to make stables of granate, and cottages of porphyry.

CHAPTER XXXIX
The adventures of Pekuah continued

'WE wandered about in this manner for some weeks, whether, as our chief pretended, for my gratification, or, as I rather suspected, for some convenience of his own. I endeavoured to appear contented where sullenness and resentment would have been of no use, and that endeavour conduced much to the calmness of my mind; but my heart was always with Nekayah, and the troubles of the night much overbalanced the amusements of the day. My women, who threw all their cares upon their mistress, set their minds at ease from the time when they saw me treated with respect, and gave themselves up to the incidental alleviations of our fatigue without solicitude[115] or sorrow. I was pleased with their pleasure, and animated with their confidence. My condition had lost much of its terrour, since I found that the Arab ranged the country merely to get riches. Avarice is an uniform and tractable vice: other intellectual distempers are different in different constitutions of mind; that which sooths the pride of one will offend the pride of another; but to the favour of the covetous there is a ready way, bring money and nothing is denied.

'At last we came to the dwelling of our chief, a strong and spacious house built with stone in an island of the Nile, which lies, as I was told, under the tropick.[116] 'Lady, said the Arab, you shall rest after your journey a few weeks in this place, where you are to consider yourself as sovereign. My occupation is war: I have therefore chosen this obscure residence, from which I can issue unexpected, and to which

I can retire unpursued. You may now repose in security: here are few pleasures, but here is no danger." He then led me into the inner apartments, and seating me on the richest couch, bowed to the ground. His women, who considered me as a rival, looked on me with malignity; but being soon informed that I was a great lady detained only for my ransome, they began to vie with each other in obsequiousness and reverence.

'Being again comforted with new assurances of speedy liberty, I was for some days diverted from impatience by the novelty of the place. The turrets overlooked the country to a great distance, and afforded a view of many windings of the stream. In the day I wandered from one place to another as the course of the sun varied the splendour of the prospect, and saw many things which I had never seen before. The crocodiles and river-horses [117] are common in this unpeopled region, and I often looked upon them with terrour, though I knew that they could not hurt me. For some time I expected to see mermaids and tritons, [118] which, as Imlac has told me, the European travellers have stationed in [119] the Nile, but no such beings ever appeared, and the Arab, when I inquired after them, laughed at my credulity.

'At night the Arab always attended me to a tower set apart for celestial observations, where he endeavoured to teach me the names and courses of the stars. I had no great inclination to this study, but an appearance of attention was necessary to please my instructor, who valued himself for his skill, and, in a little while, I found some employment requisite to beguile the tediousness of time, which was to be passed always amidst the same objects. I was weary of looking in the morning on things from which I had turned away weary in the evening: I therefore was at last willing to observe the stars rather than do nothing, but could not always compose my thoughts, and was very often thinking on Nekayah when others imagined me contemplating the sky. Soon after the Arab went upon another expedition, and then my only pleasure was to talk with my maids about the accident by which we were carried away, and the happiness that we should all enjoy at the end of our captivity.'

'There were women in your Arab's fortress, said the princess, why did you not make them your companions, enjoy their conversation, and partake their diversions? In a place where they found business or amusement, why should you alone sit corroded with idle melancholy? or why could not you bear for a few months that condition to which they were condemned for life?'

'The diversions of the women, answered Pekuah, were only childish play, by which the mind accustomed to stronger operations could not be kept busy. I could do all which they delighted in doing by powers merely sensitive,[120] while my intellectual faculties were flown to Cairo. They ran from room to room as a bird hops from wire to wire in his cage. They danced for the sake of motion, as lambs frisk in a meadow. One sometimes pretended to be hurt that the rest might be alarmed, or hid herself that another might seek her. Part of their time passed in watching the progress of light bodies that floated on the river, and part in marking the various forms into which clouds broke in the sky.

'Their business was only needlework, in which I and my maids sometimes helped them; but you know that the mind will easily straggle from the fingers, nor will you suspect that captivity and absence from Nekayah could receive solace from silken flowers.

'Nor was much satisfaction to be hoped from their conversation: for of what could they be expected to talk? They had seen nothing; for they had lived from early youth in that narrow spot: of what they had not seen they could have no knowledge, for they could not read. They had no ideas but of the few things that were within their view, and had hardly names for any thing but their cloaths and their food. As I bore a superiour character, I was often called to terminate their quarrels, which I decided as equitably as I could. If it could have amused me to hear the complaints of each against the rest, I might have been often detained by long stories, but the motives of their animosity were so small that I could not listen without intercepting[121] the tale.'

'How, said Rasselas, can the Arab, whom you represented as a man of more than common accomplishments, take any pleasure in his seraglio, when it is filled only with women like these. Are they exquisitely beautiful?'

'They do not, said Pekuah, want that unaffecting and ignoble beauty which may subsist without spriteliness or sublimity, without energy of thought or dignity of virtue. But to a man like the Arab such beauty was only a flower casually plucked and carelessly thrown away. Whatever pleasures he might find among them, they were not those of friendship or society. When they were playing about him he looked on them with inattentive superiority: when they vied for his regard he sometimes turned away disgusted. As they had no knowledge, their talk could take nothing from the tediousness of life: as they had no choice, their fondness, or appearance of fondness, excited in him neither pride nor gratitude; he was not exalted in his own esteem by the smiles of a woman who saw no other man, nor was much obliged by that regard, of which he could never know the sincerity, and which he might often perceive to be exerted not so much to delight him as to pain a rival. That which he gave, and they received, as love, was only a careless distribution of superfluous time, such love as man can bestow upon that which he despises, such as has neither hope nor fear, neither joy nor sorrow.'

'You have reason, lady, to think yourself happy, said Imlac, that you have been thus easily dismissed. How could a mind, hungry for knowledge, be willing, in an intellectual famine, to lose such a banquet as Pekuah's conversation?'

'I am inclined to believe, answered Pekuah, that he was for some time in suspense;[122] for, notwithstanding his promise, whenever I proposed to dispatch a messenger to Cairo, he found some excuse for delay. While I was detained in his house he made many incursions into the neighbouring countries, and, perhaps, he would have refused to discharge me, had his plunder been equal to his wishes. He returned always courteous, related his adventures, delighted to hear my observations, and endeavoured to advance my acquaintance with the stars. When I importuned him to send away my letters, he soothed me with professions of honour and sincerity; and, when I could be no longer decently denied, put his troop again in motion, and left me to govern in his absence. I was much afflicted by this studied procrastination, and was sometimes afraid that I should be forgotten; that you would leave Cairo, and I must end my days in an island of the Nile.

'I grew at last hopeless and dejected, and cared so little to entertain him, that he for a while more frequently talked with my maids. That he should fall in love with them, or with me, might have been equally fatal, and I was not much pleased with the growing friendship. My anxiety was not long; for, as I recovered some degree of cheerfulness, he returned to me, and I could not forbear to despise my former uneasiness.

'He still delayed to send for my ransome, and would, perhaps, never have determined, had not your agent found his way to him. The gold, which he would not fetch, he could not reject when it was offered. He hastened to prepare for our journey hither, like a man delivered from the pain of an intestine conflict. I took leave of my companions in the house, who dismissed me with cold indifference.'

Nekayah, having heard her favourite's relation, rose and embraced her, and Rasselas gave her an hundred ounces of gold, which she presented to the Arab for the fifty that were promised.

CHAPTER XL

The history of a man of learning

THEY returned to Cairo, and were so well pleased at finding themselves together, that none of them went much abroad. The prince began to love learning, and one day declared to Imlac, that he intended to devote himself to science, and pass the rest of his days in literary solitude.

'Before you make your final choice, answered Imlac, you ought to examine its hazards, and converse with some of those who are grown old in the company of themselves. I have just left the observatory of one of the most learned astronomers in the world, who has spent forty years in unwearied attention to the motions and appearances of the celestial bodies, and has drawn out his soul in endless calculations. He admits a few friends once a month to hear his deductions and enjoy his discoveries. I was introduced as a man of knowledge worthy of his notice. Men of various ideas and fluent conversation are commonly welcome to those whose thoughts have been long fixed upon a single point, and who find the images of other things stealing away. I delighted him with my remarks, he smiled at the narrative of my travels, and was glad to forget the constellations, and descend for a moment into the lower world.

'On the next day of vacation [123] I renewed my visit, and was so fortunate as to please him again. He relaxed from that time the severity of his rule, and permitted me to enter at my own choice. I found him always busy, and always glad to be relieved. As each knew much which the other was desirous of learning, we exchanged our notions with great delight. I perceived that I had every day more of his confidence, and always found new cause of admiration in the profundity of his mind. His comprehension is vast, his memory capacious and retentive, his discourse is methodical, and his expression clear.

'His integrity and benevolence are equal to his learning. His deepest researches and most favourite studies are willingly interrupted for any opportunity of doing good by his counsel or his riches. To his closest retreat, at his most busy moments, all are admitted that want his assistance: 'For though I exclude idleness and pleasure, I will never, says he, bar my doors against charity. To man is permitted the contemplation of the skies, but the practice of virtue is commanded.'

'Surely, said the princess, this man is happy.'

'I visited him, said Imlac, with more and more frequency, and was every time more enamoured of his conversation: he was sublime[124] without haughtiness, courteous without formality, and communicative without ostentation. I was at first, great princess, of your opinion, thought him the happiest of mankind, and often congratulated him on the blessing that he enjoyed. He seemed to hear nothing with indifference but the praises of his condition,[125] to which he always returned a general answer, and diverted the conversation to some other topick.

'Amidst this willingness to be pleased, and labour to please, I had quickly reason to imagine that some painful sentiment pressed upon his mind. He often looked up earnestly towards the sun, and let his voice fall in the midst of his discourse. He would sometimes, when we were alone, gaze upon me in silence with the air of a man who longed to speak what he was yet resolved to suppress. He would often send for me with vehement injunctions of haste, though, when I came to him, he had nothing extraordinary to say. And sometimes, when I was leaving him, would call me back, pause a few moments and then dismiss me.

CHAPTER XLI

The astronomer discovers the cause of his uneasiness

AT last the time came when the secret burst his reserve. We were sitting together last night in the turret of his house, watching the emersion[126] of a satellite of Jupiter. A sudden tempest clouded the sky, and disappointed our observation. We sat a while silent in the dark, and then he addressed himself to me in these words: 'Imlac, I have long considered thy friendship as the greatest blessing of my life. Integrity without knowledge is weak and useless, and knowledge without integrity is dangerous and dreadful. I have found in thee all the qualities requisite for trust, benevolence, experience, and fortitude. I have long discharged an office which I must soon quit at the call of nature, and shall rejoice in the hour of imbecility[127] and pain to devolve it upon thee.'

'I thought myself honoured by this testimony, and protested that whatever could conduce to his happiness would add likewise to mine.'

'Hear, Imlac, what thou wilt not without difficulty credit. I have possessed for five years the regulation of weather, and the distribution of the seasons: the sun has listened to my dictates, and passed from tropick to tropick by my direction; the clouds, at my call, have poured their waters, and the Nile has overflowed at my command; I have restrained the rage of the dog-star,[128] and mitigated the fervours of the crab.[129] The winds alone, of all the elemental powers, have hitherto refused my authority, and multitudes have perished by equinoctial tempests which I found myself unable to prohibit or restrain. I have administered this great office with exact justice, and made to the different nations of the earth an impartial dividend of rain and sunshine. What must have been the misery of half the globe, if I had limited the clouds to particular regions, or confined the sun to either side of the equator?'

CHAPTER XLII

The opinion of the astronomer is explained and justified

'I SUPPOSE he discovered in me, through the obscurity of the room, some tokens of amazement and doubt, for, after a short pause, he proceeded thus:

'Not to be easily credited will neither surprise nor offend me; for I am, probably, the first of human beings to whom this trust has been imparted. Nor do I know whether to deem this distinction a reward or punishment; since I have possessed it I have been far less happy than before, and nothing but the consciousness of good intention could have enabled me to support the weariness of unremitted vigilance.'

'How long, Sir, said I, has this great office been in your hands?'

'About ten years ago, said he, my daily observations of the changes of the sky led me to consider, whether, if I had the power of the seasons, I could confer greater plenty upon the inhabitants of the earth. This contemplation fastened on my mind, and I sat days and nights in imaginary dominion, pouring upon this country and that the showers of fertility, and seconding every fall of rain with a due proportion of sunshine. I had yet only the will to do good, and did not imagine that I should ever have the power.

'One day as I was looking on the fields withering with heat, I felt in my mind a sudden wish that I could send rain on the southern mountains, and raise the Nile to an inundation. In the hurry of my imagination I commanded rain to fall, and, by comparing the time of my command, with that of the inundation, I found that the clouds had listened to my lips.'

'Might not some other cause, said I, produce this concurrence? the Nile does not always rise on the same day.'

'Do not believe, said he with impatience, that such objections could escape me: I reasoned long against my own conviction, and laboured against truth with the utmost obstinacy. I sometimes suspected myself of madness, and should not have dared to impart this secret but to a man like you, capable of distinguishing the wonderful from the impossible, and the incredible from the false.'

'Why, Sir, said I, do you call that incredible, which you know, or think you know, to be true?'

'Because, said he, I cannot prove it by any external evidence; and I know too well the laws of demonstration to think that my conviction ought to influence another, who cannot, like me, be conscious of its force. I, therefore, shall not attempt to gain credit by disputation. It is sufficient that I feel this power, that I have long possessed, and every day exerted it. But the life of man is short, the infirmities of age increase upon me, and the time will soon come when the regulator of the year must mingle with the dust. The care of appointing a successor has long disturbed me; the night and the day have been spent in comparisons of all the characters which have come to my knowledge, and I have yet found none so worthy as thyself.

CHAPTER XLIII

The astronomer leaves Imlac his directions

'Hear therefore, what I shall impart, with attention, such as the welfare of a world requires. If the task of a king be considered as difficult, who has the care only of a few millions, to whom he cannot do much good or harm, what must be the anxiety of him, on whom depends the action of the elements, and the great gifts of light and heat! – Hear me therefore with attention.

'I have diligently considered the position of the earth and sun, and formed innumerable schemes in which I changed their situation. I have sometimes turned aside the axis of the earth, and sometimes varied the ecliptick of the sun: but I have found it impossible to make a disposition by which the world may be advantaged; what one region gains, another loses by any imaginable alteration, even without considering the distant parts of the solar system with which we are unacquainted. Do not, therefore, in thy administration of the year, indulge thy pride by innovation; do not please thyself with thinking that thou canst make thyself renowned to all future ages, by disordering the seasons. The memory of mischief is no desirable fame. Much less will it become thee to let kindness or interest prevail. Never rob other countries of rain to pour it on thine own. For us the Nile is sufficient.'

'I promised that when I possessed the power, I would use it with inflexible integrity, and he dismissed me, pressing my hand.' 'My heart, said he, will be now at rest, and my benevolence will no more destroy my quiet: I have found a man of wisdom and virtue, to whom I can cheerfully bequeath the inheritance of the sun.'

The prince heard this narration with very serious regard, but the princess smiled, and Pekuah convulsed herself with laughter. 'Ladies, said Imlac, to mock the heaviest of human afflictions is neither charitable nor wise. Few can attain this man's knowledge, and few practise his virtues; but all may suffer his calamity. Of the uncertainties of our present state, the most dreadful and alarming is the uncertain continuance of reason.'

The princess was recollected,[130] and the favourite was abashed. Rasselas, more deeply affected, inquired of Imlac, whether he thought such maladies of the mind frequent, and how they were contracted.

CHAPTER XLIV

The dangerous prevalence[131] *of imagination*

'DISORDERS of intellect, answered Imlac, happen much more often than superficial observers will easily believe. Perhaps, if we speak with rigorous exactness, no human mind is in its right state. There is no man whose imagination does not sometimes predominate over his reason, who can regulate his attention wholly by his will, and whose ideas will come and go at his command. No man will be found in whose mind airy[132] notions do not sometimes tyrannise, and force him to hope or fear beyond the limits of sober probability. All power of fancy over reason is a degree of insanity; but while this power is such as we can controll and repress, it is not visible to others, nor considered as any depravation of the mental faculties: it is not pronounced madness but when it comes[133] ungovernable, and apparently[134] influences speech or action.

'To indulge the power of fiction, and send imagination out upon the wing, is often the sport of those who delight too much in silent speculation. When we are alone we are not always busy; the labour of excogitation is too violent to last long; the ardour of inquiry will sometimes give way to idleness or satiety. He who has nothing external that can divert him, must find pleasure in his own thoughts, and must conceive himself what he is not; for who is pleased with what he is? He then expiatates in boundless futurity, and culls from all imaginable conditions that which for the present moment he should most desire, amuses his desires with impossible enjoyments, and confers upon his pride unattainable dominion. The mind dances from scene to scene, unites all pleasures in all combinations, and riots in delights which nature and fortune, with all their bounty, cannot bestow.

'In time some particular train of ideas fixes the attention, all other intellectual gratifications are rejected, the mind, in weariness or leisure, recurs constantly to the favourite conception, and feasts on the luscious falsehood whenever she is offended with the bitterness of truth. By degrees the reign of fancy is confirmed; she grows first imperious, and in time despotick. Then fictions begin to operate as realities, false opinions fasten upon the mind, and life passes in dreams of rapture or of anguish.

'This, Sir, is one of the dangers of solitude, which the hermit has confessed not always to promote goodness, and the astronomer's misery has proved to be not always propitious to wisdom.'

'I will no more, said the favourite, imagine myself the queen of Abissinia. I have often spent the hours, which the princess gave to my own disposal, in adjusting ceremonies and regulating the court; I have repressed the pride of the powerful, and granted the petitions of the poor; I have built new palaces in more happy situations, planted groves upon the tops of mountains, and have exulted in the beneficence of royalty, till, when the princess entered, I had almost forgotten to bow down before her.'

'And I, said the princess, will not allow myself any more to play the shepherdess in my waking dreams. I have often soothed my thoughts with the quiet and innocence of pastoral employments, till I have in my chamber heard the winds whistle, and the sheep bleat; sometimes freed the lamb entangled in the thicket, and sometimes with my crook encountered the wolf. I have a dress like that of the village maids, which I put on to help my imagination, and a pipe on which I play softly, and suppose myself followed by my flocks.'

'I will confess, said the prince, an indulgence of fantastick[135] delight more dangerous than yours. I have frequently endeavoured to image[136] the possibility of a perfect government, by which all wrong should be restrained, all vice reformed, and all the subjects preserved in tranquillity and innocence. This thought produced innumerable schemes of reformation, and dictated many useful regulations and salutary edicts. This has been the sport and sometimes the labour of my solitude; and I start, when I think with how little anguish I once supposed the death of my father and my brothers.'

'Such, says Imlac, are the effects of visionary schemes: when we first form them we know them to be absurd, but familiarise them by degrees, and in time lose sight of their folly.'

CHAPTER XLV

They discourse with an old man

THE evening was now far past, and they rose to return home. As they walked along the bank of the Nile, delighted with the beams of the moon quivering on the water, they saw at a small distance an old man, whom the prince had often heard in the assembly of the sages. 'Yonder, said he, is one whose years have calmed his passions, but not clouded his reason: let us close the disquisitions of the night, by inquiring what are his sentiments of his own state, that we may know whether youth alone is to struggle with vexation, and whether any better hope remains for the latter part of life.'

Here the sage approached and saluted them. They invited him to join their walk, and prattled[137] a while as acquaintance that had unexpectedly met one another. The old man was cheerful and talkative, and the way seemed short in his company. He was pleased to find himself not disregarded, accompanied them to their house, and, at the prince's request, entered with them. They placed him in the seat of honour, and set wine and conserves before him.

'Sir, said the princess, an evening walk must give to a man of learning, like you, pleasures which ignorance and youth can hardly conceive. You know the qualities[138] and the causes of all that you behold, the laws by which the river flows, the periods in which the planets perform their revolutions. Every thing must supply you with contemplation,[139] and renew the consciousness of your own dignity.'[140]

'Lady, answered he, let the gay and the vigorous expect pleasure in their excursions, it is enough that age can obtain ease. To me the world has lost its novelty: I look round, and see what I remember to have seen in happier days. I rest against a tree, and consider, that in the same shade I once disputed upon the annual overflow of the Nile with a friend who is now silent in the grave. I cast my eyes upwards, fix them on the changing moon, and think with pain on the vicissitudes of life. I have ceased to take much delight in physical[141] truth; for what have I to do with those things which I am soon to leave?'

'You may at least recreate[142] yourself, said Imlac, with the recollection of an honourable and useful life, and enjoy the praise which all agree to give you.'

'Praise, said the sage, with a sigh, is to an old man an empty sound. I have neither mother to be delighted with the reputation of her son, nor wife to partake the honours of her husband.[143] I have outlived my friends and my rivals. Nothing is now of much importance; for I cannot extend my interest beyond myself. Youth is delighted with applause, because it is considered as the earnest of some future good, and because the prospect of life is far extended: but to me, who am now declining to decrepitude, there is little to be feared from the malevolence of men, and yet less to be hoped from their affection or esteem. Something they may yet take away, but they can give me nothing. Riches would now be useless, and high employment would be pain. My retrospect of life recalls to my view many opportunities of good neglected, much time squandered upon trifles, and more lost in idleness and vacancy.[144] I leave many great designs unattempted, and many great attempts unfinished. My mind is burthened with no heavy crime, and therefore I compose myself to tranquillity; endeavour to abstract my thoughts from hopes and cares, which, though reason knows them to be vain, still try to keep their old possession of the heart; expect, with serene humility, that hour which nature cannot long delay; and hope to possess in a better state that happiness which here I could not find, and that virtue which here I have not attained.'

He rose and went away, leaving his audience not much elated with the hope of long life. The prince consoled himself with remarking, that it was not reasonable to be disappointed by this account; for age had never been considered as the season of felicity, and, if it was possible to be easy in decline and weakness, it was likely that the days of vigour and alacrity might be happy: that the noon of life might be bright, if the evening could be calm.

The princess suspected that age was querulous and malignant, and delighted to repress the expectations of those who had newly entered the world. She had seen the possessors of estates look with envy on their heirs, and known many who enjoy pleasure no longer than they can confine it to themselves.

Pekuah conjectured, that the man was older than he appeared, and was willing to impute his complaints to delirious dejection; or else supposed that he had been unfortunate, and was therefore discontented: 'For nothing, said she, is more common than to call our own condition, the condition of life.'

Imlac, who had no desire to see them depressed, smiled at the comforts which they could so readily procure to themselves, and remembered, that at the same age, he was equally confident of unmingled prosperity, and equally fertile of consolatory expedients. He forbore to force upon them unwelcome knowledge, which time itself would too soon impress. The princess and her lady retired; the madness of the astronomer hung upon their minds, and they desired Imlac to enter upon his office, and delay next morning the rising of the sun.

CHAPTER XLVI

The princess and Pekuah visit the astronomer

THE princess and Pekuah having talked in private of Imlac's astronomer, thought his character at once so amiable and so strange, that they could not be satisfied without a nearer knowledge, and Imlac was requested to find the means of bringing them together.

This was somewhat difficult; the philosopher had never received any visits from women, though he lived in a city that had in it many Europeans who followed the manners of their own countries, and many from other parts of the world that lived there with European liberty. The ladies would not be refused, and several schemes were proposed for the accomplishment of their design. It was proposed to introduce them as strangers in distress, to whom the sage was always accessible; but, after some deliberation, it appeared, that by this artifice, no acquaintance could be formed, for their conversation would be short, and they could not decently importune him often. 'This, said Rasselas, is true; but I have yet a stronger objection against the misrepresentation of your state. I have always considered it as treason against the great republick of human nature, to make any man's virtues the means of deceiving him, whether on great or little occasions. All imposture weakens confidence and chills benevolence. When the sage finds that you are not what you seemed, he will feel the resentment natural to a man who, conscious of great abilities, discovers that he has been tricked by understandings meaner than his own, and, perhaps, the distrust, which he can never afterwards wholly lay aside, may stop the voice of counsel, and close the hand of charity; and where will you find the power of restoring his benefactions to mankind, or his peace to himself ?'

To this no reply was attempted, and Imlac began to hope

that their curiosity would subside; but, next day, Pekuah told him, she had now found an honest pretence for a visit to the astronomer, for she would solicit permission to continue under him the studies in which she had been initiated by the Arab, and the princess might go with her either as a fellow-student, or because a woman could not decently come alone. 'I am afraid, said Imlac, that he will be soon weary of your company: men advanced far in knowledge do not love to repeat the elements of their art, and I am not certain that even of the elements, as he will deliver them connected with inferences, and mingled with reflections, you are a very capable auditress.' 'That, said Pekuah, must be my care: I ask of you only to take me thither. My knowledge is, perhaps, more than you imagine it, and by concurring always with his opinions I shall make him think it greater than it is.'

The astronomer, in pursuance of this resolution, was told, that a foreign lady, travelling in search of knowledge, had heard of his reputation, and was desirous to become his scholar. The uncommonness of the proposal raised at once his surprise and curiosity, and when, after a short deliberation, he consented to admit her, he could not stay without impatience till the next day.

The ladies dressed themselves magnificently, and were attended by Imlac to the astronomer, who was pleased to see himself approached with respect by persons of so splendid an appearance. In the exchange of the first civilities he was timorous and bashful; but when the talk became regular, he recollected[145] his powers, and justified the character which Imlac had given. Inquiring of Pekuah what could have turned her inclination towards astronomy, he received from her a history of her adventure at the pyramid, and of the time passed in the Arab's island. She told her tale with ease and elegance, and her conversation took possession of his heart. The discourse was then turned to astronomy: Pekuah displayed what she knew: he looked upon her as a prodigy of genius, and entreated her not to desist from a study which she had so happily begun.

They came again and again, and were every time more welcome than before. The sage endeavoured to amuse them, that they might prolong their visits, for he found his thoughts grow brighter in their company; the clouds of solicitude vanished by degrees, as he forced himself to entertain them, and he grieved when he was left at their departure to his old employment of regulating the seasons.

The princess and her favourite had now watched his lips for several months, and could not catch a single word from which they could judge whether he continued, or not, in the opinion of his preternatural commission. They often contrived to bring him to an open declaration, but he easily eluded all their attacks, and on which side soever they pressed him escaped from them to some other topick.

As their familiarity increased they invited him often to the house of Imlac, where they distinguished him by extraordinary respect. He began gradually to delight in sublunary pleasures. He came early and departed late; laboured to recommend himself by assiduity and compliance; excited their curiosity after new arts, that they might still want his assistance; and when they made any excursion of pleasure or inquiry, entreated to attend them.

By long experience of his integrity and wisdom, the prince and his sister were convinced that he might be trusted without danger; and lest he should draw any false hopes from the civilities which he received, discovered to him their condition, with the motives of their journey, and required his opinion on the choice of life.

'Of the various conditions which the world spreads before you, which you shall prefer, said the sage, I am not able to instruct you. I can only tell that I have chosen wrong. I have passed my time in study without experience; in the attainment of sciences which can, for the most part, be but remotely useful to mankind. I have purchased knowledge at the expence of all the common comforts of life: I have missed the endearing elegance of female friendship, and the happy commerce [146] of domestick tenderness. If I have obtained any prerogatives above other students, they have been accompanied with fear, disquiet, and scrupulosity; but even of these prerogatives, whatever they were, I have, since my thoughts have been diversified by more intercourse with the world, begun to question the reality. When I have been for a few days lost in pleasing dissipation, I am always tempted to think that my inquiries have ended in errour, and that I have suffered much, and suffered it in vain.'

Imlac was delighted to find that the sage's understanding was breaking through its mists, and resolved to detain him from the planets till he should forget his task of ruling them, and reason should recover its original influence.

From this time the astronomer was received into familiar friendship, and partook of all their projects and pleasures: his respect kept him attentive, and the activity of Rasselas did not leave much time unengaged. Something was always to be done; the day was spent in making observations which furnished talk for the evening, and the evening was closed with a scheme for the morrow.

The sage confessed to Imlac, that since he had mingled in the gay tumults of life, and divided his hours by a succession of amusements, he found the conviction of his authority over the skies fade gradually from his mind, and began to trust less to an opinion which he never could prove to others, and which he now found subject to variation from causes in which reason had no part. 'If I am accidentally left alone for a few hours, said he, my inveterate persuasion rushes upon my soul, and my thoughts are chained down by some irresistible violence, but they are soon disentangled by the prince's conversation, and instantaneously released at the entrance of Pekuah. I am like a man habitually afraid of spectres, who is set at ease by a lamp, and wonders at the dread which harassed him in the dark, yet, if his lamp be extinguished, feels again the terrours which he knows that when it is light he shall feel no more. But I am sometimes afraid lest I indulge my quiet by criminal negligence, and voluntarily forget the great charge with which I am entrusted. If I favour myself in a known errour, or am determined by my own ease in a doubtful question of this importance, how dreadful is my crime!'

'No disease of the imagination, answered Imlac, is so difficult of cure, as that which is complicated with the dread of guilt: fancy and conscience then act interchangeably upon us, and so often shift their places, that the illusions of one are not distinguished from the dictates of the other. If fancy presents images not moral or religious, the mind drives them away when they give it pain, but when melancholick notions take the form of duty, they lay hold on the faculties without opposition, because we are afraid to exclude or banish them. For this reason the superstitious are often melancholy, and the melancholy almost always superstitious.

'But do not let the suggestions of timidity overpower your better reason: the danger of neglect can be but as the probability of the obligation, which, when you consider it with freedom, you find very little, and that little growing every day less. Open your heart to the influence of the light, which, from time to time, breaks in upon you: when scruples¹⁴⁷ importune you, which you in your lucid moments know to be vain, do not stand to parley, but fly to business or to Pekuah, and keep this thought always prevalent, that you are only one atom of the mass of humanity, and have neither such virtue nor vice, as that you should be singled out for supernatural favours or afflictions.'

CHAPTER XLVII

The prince enters, and brings a new topick

'ALL this, said the astronomer, I have often thought, but my reason has been so long subjugated by an uncontrolable and overwhelming idea, that it durst not confide in its own decisions. I now see how fatally I betrayed my quiet, by suffering chimeras to prey upon me in secret; but melancholy shrinks from communication, and I never found a man before, to whom I could impart my troubles, though[148] I had been certain of relief. I rejoice to find my own sentiments confirmed by yours, who are not easily deceived, and can have no motive or purpose to deceive. I hope that time and variety will dissipate the gloom that has so long surrounded me, and the latter part of my days will be spent in peace.'

'Your learning and virtue, said Imlac, may justly give you hopes.'

Rasselas then entered with the princess and Pekuah, and inquired whether they had contrived any new diversion for the next day. 'Such, said Nekayah, is the state of life, that none are happy but by the anticipation of change: the change itself is nothing; when we have made it, the next wish is to change again. The world is not yet exhausted; let me see something to morrow which I never saw before.'

'Variety, said Rasselas, is so necessary to content, that even the happy valley disgusted me by the recurrence of its luxuries; yet I could not forbear to reproach myself with impatience, when I saw the monks of St Anthony support without complaint, a life, not of uniform delight, but uniform hardship.'

'Those men, answered Imlac, are less wretched in their silent convent than the Abissinian princes in their prison of pleasure. Whatever is done by the monks is incited by an adequate and reasonable motive. Their labour supplies them with necessaries; it therefore cannot be omitted, and is certainly rewarded. Their devotion prepares them for another state, and reminds them of its approach, while it fits them for it. Their time is regularly distributed; one duty succeeds another, so that they are not left open to the distraction of unguided choice, nor lost in the shades of listless inactivity. There is a certain task to be performed at an appropriated[149] hour; and their toils are cheerful, because they consider them as acts of piety, by which they are always advancing towards endless felicity.'

'Do you think, said Nekayah, that the monastick rule is

a more holy and less imperfect state than any other? May not he equally hope for future happiness who converses[150] openly with mankind, who succours the distressed by his charity, instructs the ignorant by his learning, and contributes by his industry to the general system of life; even though he should omit some of the mortifications which are practised in the cloister, and allow himself such harmless delights as his condition may place within his reach?'

'This, said Imlac, is a question which has long divided the wise, and perplexed the good. I am afraid to decide on either part. He that lives well in the world is better than he that lives well in a monastery. But, perhaps, every one is not able to stem the temptations of publick life; and, if he cannot conquer, he may properly retreat. Some have little power to do good, and have likewise little strength to resist evil. Many are weary of their conflicts with adversity, and are willing to eject those passions which have long busied them in vain. And many are dismissed by age and diseases from the more laborious duties of society. In monasteries the weak and timorous may be happily sheltered, the weary may repose, and the penitent may meditate. Those retreats of prayer and contemplation have something so congenial to the mind of man, that, perhaps, there is scarcely one that does not purpose to close his life in pious abstraction with a few associates serious as himself.'

'Such, said Pekuah, has often been my wish, and I have heard the princess declare, that she should not willingly die in a crowd.'

'The liberty of using[151] harmless pleasures, proceeded Imlac, will not be disputed; but it is still to be examined what pleasures are harmless. The evil of any pleasure that Nekayah can image is not in the act itself, but in its consequences. Pleasure, in itself harmless, may become mischievous, by endearing to us a state which we know to be transient and probatory,[152] and withdrawing our thoughts from that,[153] of which every hour brings us nearer to the beginning, and of which no length of time will bring us to the end. Mortification is not virtuous in itself, nor has any other use, but that it disengages us from the allurements of sense. In the state of future perfection, to which we all aspire, there will be pleasure without danger, and security without restraint.'

The princess was silent, and Rasselas, turning to the astronomer, asked him, whether he could not delay her retreat, by showing her something which she had not seen before.

'Your curiosity, said the sage, has been so general, and your pursuit of knowledge so vigorous, that novelties are not now very easily to be found: but what you can no longer procure from the living may be given by the dead. Among the wonders of this country are the catacombs, or the ancient repositories, in which the bodies of the earliest generations were lodged, and where, by the virtue of the gums which embalmed them, they yet remain without corruption.'

'I know not, said Rasselas, what pleasure the sight of the catacombs can afford; but, since nothing else is offered, I am resolved to view them, and shall place this with many other things which I have done, because I would do something.'

They hired a guard of horsemen, and the next day visited the catacombs. When they were about to descend into the sepulchral caves, 'Pekuah, said the princess, we are now again invading the habitations of the dead; I know that you will stay behind; let me find you safe when I return.' 'No, I will not be left, answered Pekuah; I will go down between you and the prince.'

They then all descended, and roved with wonder through the labyrinth of subterraneous passages, where the bodies were laid in rows on either side.

CHAPTER XLVIII

Imlac discourses on the nature of the soul

'WHAT reason, said the prince, can be given, why the Egyptians should thus expensively preserve those carcasses which some nations consume with fire, others lay to mingle with the earth, and all agree to remove from their sight, as soon as decent rites can be performed?'

'The original[154] of ancient customs, said Imlac, is commonly unknown; for the practice often continues when the cause has ceased; and concerning superstitious ceremonies it is vain to conjecture; for what reason did not dictate reason cannot explain. I have long believed that the practice of embalming arose only from tenderness to the remains of relations or friends, and to this opinion I am more inclined, because it seems impossible that this care should have been general: had all the dead been embalmed, their repositories must in time have been more spacious than the dwellings of the living. I suppose only the rich or honourable were secured from corruption, and the rest left to the course of nature.

'But it is commonly supposed that the Egyptians believed the soul to live as long as the body continued undissolved, and therefore tried this method of eluding death.'

'Could the wise Egyptians, said Nekayah, think so grossly of the soul? If the soul could once survive its separation, what could it afterwards receive or suffer from the body?'

'The Egyptians would doubtless think erroneously, said the astronomer, in the darkness of heathenism, and the first dawn of philosophy. The nature of the soul is still disputed amidst all our opportunities of clearer knowledge: some yet say, that it may be material, who, nevertheless, believe it to be immortal.'

'Some, answered Imlac, have indeed said that the soul is material, but I can scarcely believe that any man has thought it, who knew how to think; for all the conclusions of reason enforce the immateriality of mind, and all the notices of sense and investigations of science concur to prove the unconsciousness of matter.

'It was never supposed that cogitation is inherent in matter, or that every particle is a thinking being. Yet, if any part of matter be devoid of thought, what part can we suppose to think? Matter can differ from matter only in form, density, bulk, motion, and direction of motion: to which of these, however varied or combined, can consciousness be annexed? To be round or square, to be solid or fluid, to be great or little, to be moved slowly or swiftly one way or another, are modes of material existence, all equally alien from the nature of cogitation. If matter be once without thought, it can only be made to think by some new modification, but all the modifications which it can admit are equally unconnected with cogitative powers.'

'But the materialists, said the astronomer, urge that matter may have qualities with which we are unacquainted.'

'He who will determine, returned Imlac, against that which he knows, because there may be something which he knows not; he that can set hypothetical possibility against acknowledged certainty, is not to be admitted among reasonable beings. All that we know of matter is, that matter is inert, senseless and lifeless; and if this conviction cannot be opposed but by referring us to something that we know not, we have all the evidence that human intellect can admit. If that which is known may be overruled by that which is unknown, no being, not omniscient, can arrive at certainty.'

'Yet let us not, said the astronomer, too arrogantly limit the Creator's power.'

'It is no limitation of omnipotence, replied the poet, to suppose that one thing is not consistent with another, that the same proposition cannot be at once true and false, that the same number cannot be even and odd, that cogitation cannot be conferred on that which is created incapable of cogitation.'

'I know not, said Nekayah, any great use of this question. Does that immateriality, which, in my opinion, you have sufficiently proved, necessarily include eternal duration?'

'Of immateriality, said Imlac, our ideas are negative, and therefore obscure. Immateriality seems to imply a natural power of perpetual duration as a consequence of exemption from all causes of decay: whatever perishes, is destroyed by the solution of its contexture, and separation of its parts; nor can we conceive how that which has no parts, and therefore admits no solution, can be naturally corrupted or impaired.'

'I know not, said Rasselas, how to conceive any thing without extension: what is extended must have parts, and you allow, that whatever has parts may be destroyed.'

'Consider your own conceptions, replied Imlac, and the difficulty will be less. You will find substance without extension. An ideal form is no less real than material bulk: yet an ideal form has no extension. It is no less certain, when you think on a pyramid, that your mind possesses the idea[155] of a pyramid, than that the pyramid itself is standing. What space does the idea of a pyramid occupy more than the idea of a grain of corn? or how can either idea suffer laceration? As is the effect such is the cause; as thought is, such is the power that thinks; a power impassive and indiscerptible.'[156]

'But the Being, said Nekayah, whom I fear to name, the Being which made the soul, can destroy it.'

'He, surely, can destroy it, answered Imlac, since, however unperishable, it receives from a superior nature its power of duration. That it will not perish by any inherent cause of decay, or principle of corruption, may be shown by philosophy; but philosophy can tell no more. That it will not be annihilated by him that made it, we must humbly learn from higher authority.'

The whole assembly stood a while silent and collected.[157]

'Let us return, said Rasselas, from this scene of mortality. How gloomy would be these mansions of the dead to him who did not know that he shall never die; that what now acts shall continue its agency, and what now thinks shall think on for ever. Those that lie here stretched before us, the wise and the powerful of ancient times, warn us to remember the shortness of our present state: they were, perhaps, snatched away while they were busy, like us, in the choice of life.'

'To me, said the princess, the choice of life is become less important; I hope hereafter to think only on the choice of eternity.'

They then hastened out of the caverns, and, under the protection of their guard, returned to Cairo.

CHAPTER XLIX

The conclusion, in which nothing is concluded

It was now the time of the inundation of the Nile: a few days after their visit to the catacombs, the river began to rise.

They were confined to their house. The whole region being under water gave them no invitation to any excursions, and, being well supplied with materials for talk, they diverted themselves with comparisons of the different forms of life which they had observed, and with various schemes of happiness which each of them had formed.

Pekuah was never so much charmed with any place as the convent of St Anthony, where the Arab restored her to the princess, and wished only to fill it with pious maidens, and to be made prioress of the order: she was weary of expectation and disgust,[158] and would gladly be fixed in some unvariable state.

The princess thought, that of all sublunary things, knowledge was the best: she desired first to learn all sciences, and then purposed to found a college of learned women, in which she would preside, that, by conversing with the old, and educating the young, she might divide her time between the acquisition and communication of wisdom, and raise up for the next age models of prudence, and patterns of piety.

The prince desired a little kingdom, in which he might administer justice in his own person, and see all the parts of government with his own eyes; but he could never fix the limits of his dominion, and was always adding to the number of his subjects.

Imlac and the astronomer were contented to be driven along the stream of life without directing their course to any particular port.

Of these wishes that they had formed they well knew that none could be obtained. They deliberated a while what was to be done, and resolved, when the inundation should cease, to return to Abissinia.

FINIS

NOTES

1. (p. 39) The passage should not be read as an exhortation to stagnation, let alone despair, but as a warning against unreasonable, delusive or 'phantom' hopes.

2. (p. 39) 'Ras' means 'Prince'; in Father Jeronymo Lobo's *Voyage to Abyssinia* reference is made to a 'Rassela Christos', and 'Rasselach' occurs in an English version (a copy of which Johnson owned) of Job Ludolf's *Historia Aethiopica* (1681).

3. (p. 39) cf. *Rambler* 204, 29 February 1752: 'Seged, lord of Ethiopia . . . the monarch of forty nations, the distributor of the waters of the Nile . . .'

4. (p. 39) Heavy, massive.

5. (p. 39) Mechanical devices.

6. (p. 40) Like the human inhabitants themselves; cf. *Paradise Lost*: in Eden no animal preyed on another.

7. (p. 41) The emperor of Abyssinia.

8. (p. 41) Life in the outside world.

9. (p. 42) Disregarded, did not respond to.

10. (p. 42) Eagerness to please; the word probably carries something of its modern sense, reflecting Rasselas's impatience with their efforts.

11. (p. 42) At other times.

12. (p. 43) Appropriate.

13. (p. 43) Showed.

14. (p. 44) Intellectual powers.

15. (p. 44) Solitude; cf. 'lonely' below: solitary, alone.

16. (p. 48) Indulgence of the fancy.

17. (p. 49) Cage.

18. (p. 49) Because they jut out: 'the summits overhang the middle part' (p. 39).

19. (p. 50) G. J. Kolb has shown how this chapter draws on John Wilkins's *Mathematical Magick* (1648).

20. (p. 50) Including, or particularly, craftsmen.

21. (p. 50) A vehicle with sails to be driven on land by the wind.

22. (p. 51) Rarefied, thinner, as opposed to 'grosser', denser.

23. (p. 53) Lightness of weight.

24. (p. 53) Keep himself in good spirits.

25. (p. 54) The name 'Icon-Imlac' occurs in Ludolf's *Historia Aethiopica*.

26. (p. 54) The first edition has 'recited'.

27. (p. 54) cf. 'Curiosity is one of the permanent and certain characteristics of a vigorous intellect' (*Rambler* 150).

28. (p. 55) 'One of the most fruitful provinces of all the Abyssinian dominions' (Johnson's translation of Lobo's *Voyage to Abyssinia*).

29. (p. 55) Its source.

30. (p. 55) Small-minded.

31. (p. 55) Despoiled.

32. (p. 55) Ruler.

33. (p. 56) Reveal.

34. (p. 56) Perhaps the first or second definition of 'invention' given by Johnson in his *Dictionary of the English Language*: '1. Excogitation; the act or power of producing something new. 2. Discovery . . .'.

35. (p. 56) Do business.

36. (p. 56) Frugality.

37. (p. 57) Learning of any kind.

38. (p. 57) Laid under an obligation, bound.

39. (p. 57) Indian port, commercial centre during the eighteenth century.

40. (p. 58) For the sake of appearances, of feasibility.

41. (p. 58) Wonderment.

42. (p. 59) A common early form of 'Hindustan'.

43. (p. 59) At this time signifying simply 'emperor'.

44. (p. 59) Conveniences.

45. (p. 60) Referring to the public display of masterpieces of Arabic poetry.

46. (p. 61) Here, as in the succeeding antithesis between 'awfully vast' and 'elegantly little', Johnson is most likely indebted to Edmund Burke's *Philosophical Enquiry into the Origin of Our Ideas of the Sublime and the Beautiful* (1757).

47. (p. 62) Role, function.

48. (p. 62) Universal and permanent, transcending time and place.

49. (p. 62) Disregard.

50. (p. 62) cf. Shelley: 'Poets are the unacknowledged

legislators of the world' (*A Defence of Poetry*, 1821, first published in 1840). On the face of it an unexpected coincidence of Augustan and Romantic; but unexpected only on the face of it.

51. (p. 63) At this time the word usually carried a derogatory significance: extravagant, immoderate or self-deluded. cf. p. 85 : 'His discourse was . . . pious without enthusiasm'.

52. (p. 63) Native.

53. (p. 64) Christianity had been the religion of Abyssinia since the fourth century.

54. (p. 65) Government, administration.

55. (p. 67) Paid court to.

56. (p. 70) Mental excitement rather than anxiety.

57. (p. 72) Rely on.

58. (p. 72) As weary of confinement as you are.

59. (p. 73) Gloomy, dismal.

60. (p. 74) 'Ranks and conditions' (p. 76).

61. (p. 74) Rough manners.

62. (p. 75) Reduced to the level of the common people.

63. (p. 75) Trade.

64. (p. 76) Could not betray.

65. (p. 76) Those given to luxurious living.

66. (p. 77) Avoid solitude and 'the tyranny of reflection'.

67. (p. 78) Mental images, ideas.

68. (p. 79) Audience.

69. (p. 80) Sentences; cf. 'polished periods and studied sentences' (p. 81).

70. (p. 81) Restored, made up for.

71. (p. 82) Primitive, uncivilized, unlearned (cf. p. 107).

72. (p. 82) cf. 'Its form is that of a pastoral, easy, vulgar, and therefore disgusting' (*Life of Milton*), and 'A Pastoral of an hundred lines may be endured; but who will hear of sheep and goats, and myrtle bowers and purling rivulets, through five acts? Such scenes please Barbarians in the dawn of literature, and children in the dawn of life; but will be for the most part thrown away, as men grow wise, and nations grow learned' (*Life of Gay*).

73. (p. 83) Early form of 'basins'.

74. (p. 83) Showed the intention.

75. (p. 84) Pasha, governor of a province. Egypt was a province of the Turkish empire.

76. (p. 84) Revel.

77. (p. 85) See Note 51.

78. (p. 86) cf. Rousseau's *Discours sur l'origine et les fondements de l'inégalité parmi les hommes*, which had come out in 1754.

79. (p. 87) Pursuit of one aim or another.

80. (p. 89) 'He is in his twenty-sixth year at the opening of the story; he passes twenty months "in visionary bustle"; and four months "in resolving to lose no more time in idle resolves". Ten months he spent in "fruitless researches" for a means of escape; and a year with the inventor of the wings. Some months, perhaps a year, must be given to his conversations with Imlac, to digging the outlet, and to the journey to Cairo. In that town they studied the language two years before they began their "experiments upon life". That Shakespeare makes Hamlet thirty years old often raises wonder. It is more surprising that Rasselas should be represented as thirty-two' (G. B. Hill, *The History of Rasselas, Prince of Abissinia*, 1887). It may be doubted that Johnson was so arithmetically aware of the passing of Rasselas's years.

81. (p. 90) General, widespread.

82. (p. 91) Turkish soldiers, originally the Sultan's guard.

83. (p. 91) Gay, vivacious.

84. (p. 92) Patronage.

85. (p. 92) Division of labour or functions.

86. (p. 93) Alloyed, adulterated.

87. (p. 94) Testimony.

88. (p. 94) In his *Dictionary* Johnson gives 'sweetness of temper' as one definition of 'candour'.

89. (p. 94) Driven to suspect fraud in others and tempted to practise it himself.

90. (p. 97) The siege of Jerusalem by Titus in A.D. 70, which ended with the destruction of the city.

91. (p. 101) cf. *Rambler* 55: 'I now left the school, and came to live with my mamma, who considered me as an usurper that had seized the rights of a woman before they were due, and was pushing her down the precipice of age, that I might reign without a superior.'

92. (p. 101) Deduce.

93. (p. 101) Views.

94. (p. 103) Sense of smell.

95. (p. 103) Civilized.

96. (p. 105) Magnificent, splendid.

97. (p. 107) Boswell reports Johnson as saying, of the appearance of spirits after death, a question he considered of the

utmost importance, 'All argument is against it; but all belief is for it.'

98. (p. 108) Boswell says that Johnson expressed 'a particular enthusiasm with respect to visiting the wall of China'.

99. (p. 108) cf. *Adventurer* 119: 'It seems to be the great business of life to create wants as fast as they are satisfied.'

100. (p. 108) Fully provided for.

101. (p. 110) Flight, escape.

102. (p. 113) Rank.

103. (p. 113) Opportunity.

104. (p. 113) Digressions.

105. (p. 115) Eagerness to please.

106. (p. 115) Spread your attentions.

107. (p. 116) Distraction, calling away.

108. (p. 118) Founder of Christian monasticism, born in Middle Egypt *c.* 250, and famous for his temptations; the monastery, Der Mar Antonius, is near the Red Sea.

109. (p. 119) Presumably an oasis, somewhat anglicized.

110. (p. 120) Abraham's son by Hagar: 'He will be a wild man; his hand will be against every man, and every man's hand against him . . .' (Genesis xvi, 12). cf. p. 60: 'a nation at once pastoral and warlike . . .'

111. (p. 121) *Laissez-passer*, safe conduct.

112. (p. 121) Scrupulousness.

113. (p. 121) Nomadic.

114. (p. 121) Traveller.

115. (p. 122) Anxiety.

116. (p. 122) Of Cancer.

117. (p. 123) Hippopotamuses.

118. (p. 123) Represented as having the head and trunk of a man and the tail of a fish, and carrying a trumpet made of a shell.

119. (p. 123) Ascribed to.

120. (p. 124) In the sense defined by Johnson in his *Dictionary* as 'having sense or perception, but not reason'; not involving the mind. cf. below: 'the mind will easily straggle from the fingers'.

121. (p. 125) Interrupting.

122. (p. 125) Undecided.

123. (p. 127) Free day.

124. (p. 128) Of superior mind or lofty bearing.

125. (p. 128) Way of life.

126. (p. 129) 'The time when a star, having been obscured by its too near approach to the sun, appears again' (Johnson's *Dictionary*).

127. (p. 129) Senility.

128. (p. 129) The Romans thought that the heat of July and August, the 'dog-days', resulted from the rising together of Sirius, the dog-star, and the sun. Pestilence and madness were associated with the dog-days.

129. (p. 129) The heat of Cancer, fourth sign of the zodiac, considered as governing the period 22 June to 22 July.

130. (p. 132) Restored to a state of composure.

131. (p. 133) Mastery.

132. (p. 133) Fanciful, unreal.

133. (p. 133) Becomes.

134. (p. 133) Obviously, manifestly.

135. (p. 134) Arising out of fantasy, unreal.

136. (p. 134) Imagine, picture.

137. (p. 135) Chatted casually.

138. (p. 135) Properties.

139. (p. 136) Matter for contemplation.

140. (p. 136) Advancement in knowledge, and thus superiority.

141. (p. 136) Concerning that which exists physically as opposed to the metaphysical or spiritual.

142. (p. 136) Refresh, divert.

143. (p. 136) Johnson's wife had died seven years before; and cf. *Idler* 41, probably written shortly after his mother's death: 'What is success to him that has none to enjoy it? Happiness is not found in self-contemplation; it is perceived only when it is reflected from another.'

144. (p. 136) Listlessness, inactivity.

145. (p. 139) Gathered.

146. (p. 140) Intercourse.

147. (p. 142) i.e. unnecessary, futile or morbid scruples.

148. (p. 143) i.e. even though.

149. (p. 143) Fixed.

150. (p. 144) Keeps company with, partakes of the life of.

151. (p. 144) Enjoying

152. (p. 144) Testing, trying us.

153. (p. 144) i.e. that state, the life after death, eternity.

154. (p. 146) Origin.

155. (p. 148) Mental image.

156. (p. 148) Incapable of, and hence not destructible by, the dissolution of its parts.

157. (p. 148) Reverentially composed, after the thought just expressed.

158. (p. 149) Disappointment.

FOR THE BEST IN PAPERBACKS, LOOK FOR THE

In every corner of the world, on every subject under the sun, Penguin represents quality and variety – the very best in publishing today.

For complete information about books available from Penguin – including Puffins, Penguin Classics and Arkana – and how to order them, write to us at the appropriate address below. Please note that for copyright reasons the selection of books varies from country to country.

In the United Kingdom: Please write to *Dept E.P., Penguin Books Ltd, Harmondsworth, Middlesex, UB7 0DA.*

If you have any difficulty in obtaining a title, please send your order with the correct money, plus ten per cent for postage and packaging, to *PO Box No 11, West Drayton, Middlesex*

In the United States: Please write to *Dept BA, Penguin, 299 Murray Hill Parkway, East Rutherford, New Jersey 07073*

In Canada: Please write to *Penguin Books Canada Ltd, 2801 John Street, Markham, Ontario L3R 1B4*

In Australia: Please write to the *Marketing Department, Penguin Books Australia Ltd, P.O. Box 257, Ringwood, Victoria 3134*

In New Zealand: Please write to the *Marketing Department, Penguin Books (NZ) Ltd, Private Bag, Takapuna, Auckland 9*

In India: Please write to *Penguin Overseas Ltd, 706 Eros Apartments, 56 Nehru Place, New Delhi, 110019*

In the Netherlands: Please write to *Penguin Books Netherlands B.V., Postbus 3507, 1001 AH, Amsterdam*

In West Germany: Please write to *Penguin Books Ltd, Friedrichstrasse 10–12, D–6000 Frankfurt/Main 1*

In Spain: Please write to *Alhambra Longman S.A., Fernandez de la Hoz 9, E–28010 Madrid*

In Italy: Please write to *Penguin Italia s.r.l., Via Como 4, I-20096 Pioltello (Milano)*

In France: Please write to *Penguin Books Ltd, 39 Rue de Montmorency, F-75003 Paris*

In Japan: Please write to *Longman Penguin Japan Co Ltd, Yamaguchi Building, 2–12–9 Kanda Jimbocho, Chiyoda-Ku, Tokyo 101*

FOR THE BEST IN PAPERBACKS, LOOK FOR THE 🐧

PENGUIN CLASSICS